# DADS + DATING = DISASTER

A moment later Mr. Wheeler came out of the house. He wasn't exactly smiling, but he wasn't frowning either. Scotti crossed her fingers and prayed that her plan would work.

Cary went into action. He reached out for the door handle, but it was obviously farther away than he had thought. He leaned past Scotti and suddenly tripped on the curb, bumping against her and pinning her to the side of the car with all of his weight.

Everything happened in a flash for Scotti. At the same instant that Cary seemed to grab her in a giant hug, her father's mouth dropped open and his face clouded up in a frown.

"What's going on?" he shouted. "Cary Calheim! Get away from my daughter!"

# The Great Dad Disaster

## Betsy Haynes

A SKYLARK BOOK

NEW YORK · TORONTO · LONDON · SYDNEY · AUCKLAND

RL5.0, 008-012

THE GREAT DAD DISASTER

A Skylark Book / June 1994

Skylark Books is a registered trademark of Bantam Books,
a division of Bantam Doubleday Dell Publishing Group, Inc.
Registered in U.S. Patent and Trademark Office and elsewhere.

ISBN 0-553-48169-X

Published simultaneously in the United States and Canada

Bantam Books are published by Bantam Books, a division of Bantam Doubleday
Dell Publishing Group, Inc. Its trademark, consisting of the words "Bantam
Books" and the portrayal of a rooster, is Registered in U.S. Patent and
Trademark Office and in other countries. Marca Registrada. Bantam Books,
1540 Broadway, New York, New York 10036.

PRINTED IN THE UNITED STATES OF AMERICA

OPM        0 9 8 7 6 5 4 3 2 1

# The
# Great Dad
# Disaster

# 1

Scotti Wheeler skidded her bike to a stop in the driveway and burst into the house, giddy with happiness.

"He asked me out! He asked me out! Cary Calheim just asked me out!" she sang at the top of her lungs as she shoved a gallon of milk into the fridge and danced around the kitchen.

The instant Dad gets home I'm going to give him a humongous hug and tell him that he's the most wonderful dad on earth, she thought.

If her father hadn't left that note asking her to ride her bike to the dairy store for milk after school, and if she hadn't taken her favorite route home from the store past Cary's house—even though it was three blocks out of the way—it might never have happened. It had helped that Cary was always in the garage after school, working on the old Mustang that he was rebuilding for when he turned sixteen next year and got his driver's license, and that he just happened to look up and see her stopped in front of his house pretending to adjust the gears on her bike. He had come out to see if she needed help, and they talked and talked until he finally asked if she would like to go to a movie with him Friday night. It was just like the plot of a romance novel.

"And I said YES! YES!" she shouted, punching the air with a fist.

I've got to call Lorna, she thought with a start, grabbing the wall phone near the kitchen sink and punching in the number. Lorna Markham had been Scotti's best friend ever since the Wheelers had moved to Texas and bought the house right behind the Markhams' when the girls were in fourth grade. Scotti and Lorna did absolutely everything together, and Scotti's father liked to make up silly names for the two of them, like The Cloneheads or The Two Stooges.

Sometimes Scotti thought it was odd that they were such close friends since they were so different in looks and personality. She was a mere four feet eleven and three-quarters inches tall with blond hair and blue eyes, while Lorna was five seven and had long dark hair. Scotti was outgoing to the point of being zany sometimes, and Lorna was quiet and shy. Scotti wanted to be a writer when she grew up, and she had already written two romance novels, starring herself as the heroine. Lorna's big ambition was to be short!

Mrs. Markham answered. "Why, hello there, Scotti," she said in her soft Texas accent. "I'm sorry, but Lorna's not here. She rode her bike to the library, and I could have sworn she said she was going to stop by your house and see if you wanted to go along."

"I must have missed her," said Scotti. "I was running an errand for my dad."

"I'll send her scooting through the back fence just as soon as she gets home," promised Mrs. Markham.

Scotti thanked her and hung up, disappointed. She couldn't wait to tell Lorna the news. Still, the Markhams' and Wheelers' backyards were only separated by a tall stockade fence with a gate in it, and Lorna would be able to get to Scotti's house almost as quickly as she could return her call.

The soft whirring sound of the garage door opening interrupted her thoughts. Her dad was home.

Captain Craig Wheeler was an airline pilot, and Scotti's mother, Helene, was a flight attendant for the same airline. They each worked three days and were off four, and they planned their work schedules so that one of them was always home with Scotti. Mrs. Wheeler had left around noon from the Dallas–Fort Worth International Airport on the New York City run.

Scotti bounced on her toes with excitement. She could hardly wait to tell her dad the terrific news. Cary Calheim had asked her for a date!

"Hi, sweetheart," said her father, coming through the door from the garage. "How's my little girl today?"

"Dad, you'll never guess what happened," Scotti began, the words tumbling out in her excitement. "This boy—his name is Cary Calheim and he goes to my school—he asked me to go to the movies with him tomorrow night. Can I go, Dad? Oh, please, *please* say yes!"

"Whoa! Hold on!" he said, looking surprised. "Would you run that by me again, a little more slowly, please?"

"Sure, Dad." She took a deep breath, trying to control the excitement in her voice. "There's this really nice boy that I met at school named Cary Calheim. We've been talking a lot, and today when I was coming home from getting the milk, we talked again, and he asked me to go to the movies with him tomorrow night. I know you'll like him. Please say I can go."

# THE GREAT DAD DISASTER

Her father gave her a skeptical look. "A date with a boy? You're kidding, aren't you?"

"Of course not," Scotti said indignantly. "Why would you think I'm kidding?"

Mr. Wheeler smiled in amusement. "Sweetheart, you're far too young to go on dates with boys. Why, I didn't expect to hear anything like this until you were at least in high school."

Scotti was thunderstruck. "But, Daaa-aaad!" she agonized, looking at him with pleading eyes. "How can you possibly say that? Nobody else's father thinks eighth grade is too young to go out with boys. You should see all the girls who have boyfriends."

"Does Lorna have a boyfriend?" he asked.

"Uh . . . she doesn't have one . . . not yet, anyway," Scotti fumbled. "But there is a boy she likes," she added, trying to save the situation.

Mr. Wheeler ruffled her hair playfully and put an arm around her. "Let's sit down and talk about this," he said, leading her to the sofa. "Tell me about this boy who has asked my little girl to go out on a date."

"Oh, Dad, I know you're going to like him," Scotti began eagerly. "He's fifteen and he's rebuilding this car in his garage to have when he turns sixteen and gets his driver's license and—"

"Whoa, again!" her father said, holding up

his hand. His face had turned to stone. "I don't like this business about a car. Don't think for one minute that you're going to be going in cars with boys for a long, long time."

"But, Dad, he's just rebuilding it. He's not driving it," she insisted. "Please say I can go. I'll absolutely die if I have to tell him that my father says I'm too young to go out with boys. He'll think I'm *a baby*." She rolled her eyes to emphasize her exasperation.

"Now, Scotti," her father said in a warning tone, "don't be in such a hurry. You've got plenty of time to date. After all, you just turned fourteen last month."

"Does that mean I can't go?" she asked in a tiny voice.

"That's right," said her father. "I meant it when I said you're too young to go out with boys, especially with one who's a year older than you and practically driving."

Scotti watched him get up from the sofa and leave the room. She was too stunned to respond.

Usually Scotti loved it when her mom was flying and she and her dad had the house to themselves. Her mother was a health nut, and when she was home they ate nothing but perfectly nutritious and totally gross things such as tofu and bean sprouts. When Scotti and her dad were in charge of the kitchen, they led a secret life, gobbling up junk food and drinking carbonated beverages to their hearts' content.

Their little conspiracy extended to housework, too. They turned into happy, carefree slobs for three days, dashing around straightening their mess in the last few minutes before Mrs. Wheeler returned home. But things were different this time.

I wish Mom were here right now instead of Dad, Scotti thought, biting her lip to hold back tears. She'd understand how embarrassing it is to have a dad who treats you like a baby and won't let boys get near you. The worst part is, she just left! She won't be back for two whole days. And Cary asked me to go out tomorrow night!

Scotti headed dejectedly for her room. She loved her room, and just walking in usually perked up her spirits. Each of the four walls was painted a different pastel color, sunny yellow, pale pink, soft green, and baby blue. The four colors were picked up as stripes in the white ruffled curtains and bedspread, and a feathery asparagus fern hung in front of the window. Her room made her think of springtime, but right now she was too miserable to notice.

The diary Lorna had given her for her birthday last month lay on her desk. It was locked, of course, and she fished the key out of its hiding place in an old sneaker in the back of her closet and unlocked it, opening it to the first page and sighing deeply.

## TUESDAY, SEPTEMBER 7

*Dear Diary,*
*Today was the first day of school, and I finally made it to eighth grade. So what? Big deal. I don't have very many classes with my friends. I don't even know why I started this stupid diary. My life is totally boring.*

She read on.

## WEDNESDAY, SEPTEMBER 8

*Dear Diary,*
*Today I saw HIM!!! He is the most gorgeous boy in the entire universe! He has dark brown hair, big brown eyes, and this incredible dimple that appears in his chin like magic when he smiles. I could stare at that chin for hours. Days, maybe.*
*I'm dying to find out his name!!*
*P.S. I love school.*

# THE GREAT DAD DISASTER

## THURSDAY, SEPTEMBER 9

*Dear Diary,*
*Today at school I saw HIM three and a half times. Once he was going into the media center. The second time was in the cafeteria. The third time he was at his locker after school. The half was when I thought I saw him ahead of me in the hall between classes, but I couldn't be positive it was really him.*
*I'm going berserk! I still don't know his name!*

Scotti glanced up and stared into space for a moment. Had that only been a week ago?

## FRIDAY, SEPTEMBER 10

*Dear Diary,*
*I found out a little bit about him today. His name is Cary Calheim, and he's in ninth grade. I looked in the phone book, and there's only one Calheim listed, so it must be him. He lives at 1407 Rolling Hills Road. That's only four blocks away! Since tomorrow's Saturday, I'm going to*

*find some excuse to go past his house*
*if it's the last thing I do!*

Scotti knew the rest of the pages by heart. It was all about how she and Lorna had biked past his house the next morning and discovered him rebuilding an old 1966 Mustang in the garage. He had invited them in to look at it, and they had started talking. They had talked more and more each day. And then today it finally happened—the most wonderful moment of her life *and the worst.*

Vaguely she was aware of the telephone ringing, but she was too miserable to pick up the extension in her room.

An instant later there was a tap at her door. "It's for you, sweetheart," said her father. "It's Lorna."

"Thank goodness," Scotti mumbled. If she had ever needed to unload to her best friend, it was now.

"Hi, Lorna. Am I ever glad—"

"Scotti! Guess what? I couldn't take the time to come over. I had to call you and tell you my news instantly!" Lorna shrieked. "Mike Kilpatrick was at the library, and he asked me to go to a movie with him tomorrow night!"

Scotti tried to answer, but the words stuck in

10

her throat. "That's great," she finally managed to get out. "Have you asked your parents if it's okay?"

"Yes. They not only said it's okay, but Daddy even gave me a big hug and said he guessed his little girl is growing up. Isn't that fantastic?"

"Yeah, it really is," Scotti said just above a whisper. "My dad's calling. I have to go now."

She hung up as tears of jealousy began to gather in her eyes.

# 2

"**I** don't have anything to wear tonight!" Lorna shrieked into the closet. "Absolutely *nothing!*"

She pawed furiously through the hangers, grabbing outfit after outfit, giving each a quick look, and pitching it onto the bed in disgust. Her big date with Mike was tonight and she had absolutely nothing to wear. Her favorite navy-blue bell-bottoms were too short now that she had shot up another half inch over the summer. Her short vintage dress would be perfect, except that the matching ribbed tights had a run. Her drawstring pajama pants were too flashy, and besides, the stripes ran up and down, making her look nine feet tall. Everything else was either hopelessly outdated or had spots that wouldn't come out or something equally horrendous.

She pushed the pile of discarded clothing to

one side and sank down on the bobbing water bed to gaze around her room and think about the situation. Her eyes swept over the bluebonnets in her wallpaper, the map of the Lone Star State over her bed, and the collection of horse statues on her dresser, but nowhere was there a clue about what she could wear on her date.

Dragging herself to her feet, she ran a brush through her long dark hair, buckled on her belt bag, and trudged down the stairs to the kitchen where the rest of the family was having breakfast. Her older brother Skip was standing at the sink, gulping down a glass of milk and snapping his fingers to the beat of a rap song playing in his head. Tiffany, who was seven, was jabbing her cereal with a spoon, trying to sink the animal shapes in the milk. But it was her parents she was interested in seeing. They were sitting at the table, drinking coffee and working crossword puzzles.

"Mom, Dad, what am I going to do? I don't have one single thing to wear tonight! It's my first date with Mike, and I'm going to look awful!"

Skip glanced at her, and an eyebrow shot up. He put his empty glass on the sink, grinning slyly. "It's my first date with Mike, and I'm going to look awful," he mimicked in a high-pitched voice as he dashed for the back door.

"Shut up, Skip," Lorna snapped and then looked imploringly at her mother. "What am I going to do, Mom?"

Mrs. Markham put down her pencil and gave her daughter a weary look. "Lorna, you have a whole closet full of beautiful clothes. Surely you can find something nice to wear."

"I know what you could wear," offered Tiffany. She grinned up at Lorna, and her missing front tooth made her look like a jack-o'-lantern with a milk mustache.

Lorna ignored Tiffany and shook her head firmly. "No, I can't, Mom. Come up to my room, and I'll show you. Honest."

"You could wear that lacy pink dress with the bows you wore when you were in Aunt Missy's wedding," offered Tiffany. "It's beautiful!"

"Tiff, would you stay out of this? That's *not* the kind of thing you wear to a movie on Friday night," Lorna said. "Mom, what am I going to do? I'm going to look *awful!*"

"Hey, little darlin', you couldn't look awful if you tried," Coy Markham drawled softly. "Come here and give your ol' daddy a good morning hug."

"Sorry, Dad," she said, bending to hug him. "It's just that tonight is the biggest night of my life, and I really want to look nice."

# THE GREAT DAD DISASTER

Mr. Markham smiled at his daughter affectionately. "My goodness, you're sure growing up fast. A big important date tonight. Why, in no time at all you'll be getting all dressed up for proms, and giving my hugs to somebody else." He made a fist with his free hand and tapped it gently on his chest. "I don't mind telling you that it gets me in the old ticker. Tugs at my heart strings just to think about it."

"I'd never give your hugs to anyone else," Lorna murmured, blushing slightly. "You know that." Across the table Tiffany giggled.

"Sure, I know," he said. "And I also think it would be a good idea for you to have something new for such a special night." He pulled a money clip out of his pants pocket and peeled a couple of bills off the roll, handing them to Lorna. Winking at Mrs. Markham, he said to Lorna, "Here you go, darlin'. Just don't tell your mother."

"Wow, Dad. Thanks a million." Lorna gave him a quick kiss on the cheek and then gave her mother one, too. Heading out the door to catch the school bus she couldn't help thinking what great parents she had. If only they weren't so tall!

Scotti wasn't at the bus stop yet when Lorna got there, so she gazed off into the distance and thought about Mike again. He was the most gorgeous boy on the face of the earth with his deep-set dark eyes and honey-blond hair, which was probably part of the reason he had just been elected captain of the school's cheerleading squad. She had watched the tryouts in awe of his gymnastic ability, and he had gotten a standing ovation from the crowd when he finished his routine.

He was also in her math class *and* her study hall. She would never forget the first day of school, when he took the seat right beside her in math. The next day he borrowed a piece of paper from her, and when she handed it to him, he gave her a dreamy smile. Of course she had been afraid to say anything to him at first, thinking that she might make an idiot of herself or that her lips would go numb and the words would come out weird. Or that maybe she wouldn't be able to talk at all. But now all that had changed.

Lorna saw Scotti approaching the bus stop.

"Hi," she called out happily. "Guess what. Dad just gave me some money to buy a new outfit for my date tonight. Isn't that cool? I've got the most fabulous dad in the world! Let's go to the mall after school, okay?"

Scotti looked up at Lorna soberly, shielding her eyes from the sun with a hand. "Can't."

"Why not?" asked Lorna.

"My dad left me a list of chores to do after school," Scotti replied crisply.

# THE GREAT DAD DISASTER

"Tomorrow's Saturday. Can't you call him and ask him if you can do them in the morning? This is so important. I really need you to help me pick out the right thing. I'll die if I don't make a perfect impression on Mike. I want him to ask me out again."

Scotti shook her head. "Dad wouldn't go for it."

Lorna was puzzled. Scotti was a genius at getting out of chores at home. And she was acting funny this morning. Like something was wrong. Maybe she just needed cheering up.

"Just think," Lorna began, "I have a date with Mike tonight, and Cary has been paying a lot of attention to you. Maybe by this time next week we'll both have dates and we can double! Wouldn't that be fabulous?"

Scotti whirled away, and Lorna thought she saw tears shoot into Scotti's eyes.

"What's wrong?" asked Lorna. "Are you mad at me? What did I say?"

When Scotti didn't answer, Lorna started to panic.

"Scotti, please tell me what's wrong," she insisted.

Scotti turned slowly around, her eyes brimming with tears. "Cary asked me to go to the movies with him tonight, too, but we can't double because my dad won't let me go. He said I'm too young to date." She threw Lorna an angry look. "*That's* why I don't want to go to the mall with you and watch you pick out new clothes for your big date with Mike. I don't even want to hear about it!" Scotti spun around again and stomped down the sidewalk.

Lorna hurried after her. "But . . . Scotti . . ." she sputtered. "I mean . . . that's awful. I didn't know, and I'm really sorry."

Just then the school bus turned the corner and rumbled to a stop beside them.

"Just leave me alone, okay?" Scotti called over her shoulder, racing up the steps and into the noisy bus.

Lorna followed, her heart aching. "Scotti, don't be mad at me," she shouted, trying to be heard over the other kids. "It's not my fault your dad won't let you go."

When she got inside the bus, she looked quickly at the pair of seats near the front where she and Scotti always sat. They were empty. Scotti was four rows back, sitting with Brianna Chambers and talking up a storm, as if the two of them were the ones who were best friends.

Lorna sank into her regular seat. She knew her face was red. But that was only part of it. Her heart was sinking into the pit of her stomach like a big cold rock.

# 3

"**M**ind if I sit with you, Brianna?" Scotti asked, looking around for an empty seat on the school bus. She knew Lorna would be hurt that she had passed up their usual seats, but she couldn't look Lorna in the eye right now. She was too upset.

Brianna looked pleased. "Sure. Lorna sick this morning?"

Scotti shook her head but didn't answer. She could see Lorna boarding the bus now and looking around for her. Turning quickly to Brianna, she plastered a fake smile on her face and said, "So, how do you like school this year? Any cute boys in your classes?"

"Are you kidding," Brianna said glumly. "This year is the pits. No cute boys and horrible teachers. I've got *Mr. Bishop* for math."

"Oh, yuck," Scotti said sympathetically.

She tried to make conversation with Brianna for the rest of the ride to school, but it was hard. Her mind was spinning. She knew it wasn't Lorna's fault that *her* father was more under-standing than her own, but that didn't help.

Since Lorna was nearer to the front of the bus, she got off first, and she was halfway to the building by the time Scotti got off.

Scotti plodded toward the school, feeling miserable. She was going to have to find Cary and tell him the bad news. How could she face him? What would she say? That she was too much of a baby to go out on a date?

What would the heroine of a romance novel do at a time like this? she asked herself. She thought back to the two novels she had written, *Prisoner of Fate* and *Journey to the Stars,* but there was nothing in either of them that could help her now. The plots were completely differ-ent from the fix she was in.

Her eyes darted to the traffic light two blocks away. She couldn't cut school and go home be-cause her dad was there. But she could board the city bus at that corner, ride to the mall, and spend the day roaming through the stores. Then she wouldn't have to face Cary or Lorna or anyone. And she just might figure out what to do about her dad.

# THE GREAT DAD DISASTER

Glancing around quickly to make sure no one was watching, she dashed up the street.

So far, so good, she thought as she hurried along.

A block from the school a red convertible with its top up screeched to a stop beside the curb. Out of the corner of her eye she could see two teenage boys in the front seat, and the one on the passenger side was rolling down his window. She hurried on, her heart beating furiously.

"Hey, Scotti. You're going in the wrong direction. What's the big idea?"

"Cary?" she said, her head snapping in the car's direction. "What are you doing driving!"

Cary opened the driver's door and got out. He crossed his arms on the roof of the car and grinned at her. His dimple made a crater in his chin the size of a dime.

"Didn't I tell you I've got my learner's permit?" he asked casually. "I got it the day I turned fifteen, and I can drive as long as I have a licensed driver in the front seat with me. This is my brother, Rex," he said, gesturing to the other boy. "It's his car. Every morning he lets me drive it this far, and then he takes it on to the high school."

"Wow," was all Scotti could say. It almost blew her mind to think that Cary could actually drive. Recovering herself, she looked quickly at his brother. "Oh, hi, Rex. Um . . . nice car."

Rex looked a lot like Cary, except he didn't have that fabulous dimple, and the red convertible was totally cool. *Beyond* cool!

Rex laughed. "It's going to look a lot nicer when my dorky brother finishes washing and waxing it after school."

She looked questioningly at Cary.

He shrugged. "Yeah, Rex is going to the movies with his girlfriend tonight, too. He said that if I'll wash the car this afternoon, they'll meet us at Rudy's after the show and we can take it around the block a couple of times. You know, show off his wheels while everybody's hanging out and watching us."

Scotti's mouth dropped open. "We, meaning . . . ?" She let the question hang in the air and pointed first at Cary and then at herself.

"Yup," he said with a cocky grin.

Her eyes popped open. "But . . . but I'm not a licensed driver. I mean, how can—"

"Hey, chill out, okay. Rex will be in the front seat with us to make it legal. But that won't matter. It'll still be fun."

She stared at him for a second, and then her mind filled with a fabulous vision of herself sitting in the front seat of Cary's brother's gorgeous red convertible and cruising around in front of all the other kids from their school! She could just imagine how they would stare. Suddenly she remembered the scene with her father. He had not only said she couldn't go on the date, but he had totally freaked at the idea of her getting into a car with a boy.

"I'd better head for school now," Rex was saying. He scooted into the driver's seat and revved the engine.

Scotti watched the car head down the street, feeling as if a gigantic hand was squeezing her heart.

There are two things that I want more than anything else in the world, Scotti thought. To go out with Cary Calheim tonight, and to ride in his brother's car. There has *got* to be some way I can convince Dad to let me go. There *has* to be!

When the red convertible had disappeared around the corner, Cary sauntered over to her, and they walked slowly toward school together.

"So, did your dad say it was okay for you to go out with me tonight?" Cary asked.

Scotti hesitated and bit her lower lip. This was it. Decision time. She had missed her chance to skip school, and now she would have to tell Cary the truth or pray that she could work things out with her dad by tonight.

The picture flashed into her mind again of the two of them cruising up and down in front of Rudy's. Smiling up at him, she took a deep breath and said brightly, "No problem."

The instant the words were out of her mouth, she started to panic. The movie started at seven P.M. It was now eight-twenty in the morning.

That meant she had exactly ten hours and forty minutes to work a miracle.

# 4

It took Lorna three tries to get the right combination for her locker. She knew her combination, of course. It was just that she hadn't been able to think straight ever since Scotti blew up at her at the bus stop and then sat with Brianna Chambers on the bus. It had hurt. A lot.

She jerked open the locker door and got out the books she needed for her morning classes, still fuming.

"Who does she think she is, blowing me off because my dad will let me go on a date and hers won't!" Lorna mumbled.

The way she saw it, she had two choices. She could break her date with Mike and stay home so that Scotti wouldn't be jealous. Or she could find a way herself to convince Mr. Wheeler to let Scotti go out with Cary.

"What a choice," she mumbled under her breath.

Scotti's dad definitely is strict, Lorna thought. I found that out when we swapped families.

Lorna was remembering last summer when she and Scotti had decided they got along better with each other's mother than they did with their own. They had persuaded their parents to let them live in each other's houses for a while. They had laughingly named their adventure the Great Mom Swap, but as it turned out, they had to adjust to new dads, too.

Lorna gently closed the locker and leaned against it, sighing. But how can I convince Mr. Wheeler, if Scotti can't? She's his own daughter.

The alternative was even worse: break her date with Mike. How could she explain it to him so that he would understand? she wondered. Would he ever ask her out again?

She tried to picture her life without Scotti. The long talks when they shared secrets. The midnight giggling sessions when they spent the night together. The emergency phone calls when one of them had a problem. Had Scotti forgotten how important they were to each other? Didn't she remember how special it was to have a best friend?

"Well, *I* haven't!" she said out loud, startling a boy walking by. He swiveled around and gave her a puzzled look.

# THE GREAT DAD DISASTER

I'm going to find Mike and make up some excuse why I can't go out tonight—but only tonight, she thought. It has to be an emergency—a temporary solution until I can talk some sense into Scotti.

She thought over several possibilities. I could tell him I'm sick. No, she decided. I don't like that one.

She chewed her bottom lip and thought some more. I could say my parents had already made plans for the whole family. She shook her head at that one, too. I would have known about it before now, she thought.

I've got it, she thought. I can tell him my parents just found out that they have this big, important dinner they have to go to and I have to baby-sit Tiff. I'll tell him they won't allow me to have company when I'm sitting. Surely he can't get mad about that.

Lorna hurried down the hall, keeping a sharp lookout for Mike. She would tell him immediately, before she lost her nerve. I've found a way to save my friendship with Scotti *and* keep my boyfriend, she thought happily.

Even so, Lorna had her fingers crossed.

When Scotti and Cary said good-bye at the front door, she hurried through the maze of hallways to the eighth-grade lockers. She needed help figuring out what to do about her dad, and she needed it badly. Lorna was the only one who could help her. If anyone could.

Thank goodness for best friends, she thought, but when she reached Lorna's locker, Lorna wasn't there.

"Darn," Scotti muttered under her breath.

"Looking for Lorna?"

Cindi Cerrone had the locker next to Lorna's. When Scotti nodded, she said, "She was here, but she cut out a few minutes ago as if her shoes were on fire."

"Which way did she go?" Scotti asked.

Cindi pointed down the hall.

"Thanks," Scotti murmured.

Glancing at her watch, she realized that she only had a couple of minutes to go to her own locker before the bell rang. There wouldn't be time to find Lorna until lunch period. In the meantime, she was on her own to think of a way to convince her dad to let her go out with Cary.

Lorna sat through her first class of the morning without hearing a word uttered by Mrs. DeLuca, her Spanish teacher. She had done it. She had broken her date with Mike.

It had been hard. She wasn't very good at lying. The instant she saw him standing beside the drinking fountain talking to a couple of guys, she had almost lost her nerve. But he saw her before she had a chance to retreat.

"Hey, Lorna," he called out, sprinting toward her. "Did you ask your parents if you can go out with me tonight?"

She nodded but didn't say anything. A lump the size of a tennis ball was stuck in her throat.

"Great. So what did they say?"

"Um . . ." she began, not wanting to say the words and yet knowing she had to. She took a deep breath and spit it out.

"They said I have to baby-sit my little sister." The words came out in a rush. "They said they're sorry and that I can go another time, but they had already made plans." She knew her face was red, and she wondered if he could tell that she was lying.

"Oh," said Mike. Disappointment clouded his face. "Well . . . I mean . . . do you think they'd mind if I came over and kept you company?"

Lorna's heart was breaking. "They don't allow me to have company when I sit. I'm sorry. I really am. And I hope you'll ask me out again." She put all the sincerity she could into those last words.

He didn't answer for an agonizing moment.

Then a sunny smile broke over his face. "Okay, how about next Friday night? Do you think they'll let you go then?"

"You bet," Lorna assured him. "My parents are really terrific. I can't wait for you to meet them."

Now, sitting in her Spanish class, she had to struggle to hold back the tears. Her big date with Mike Kilpatrick was on hold for an entire week.

I hope Scotti appreciates what I've done, Lorna thought. I hope saving our friendship was worth it.

Scotti was relieved to see Lorna's head towering above several kids in the lunch line ahead of her. She could never convince Lorna how lucky she was to be tall and easy to spot. It was especially lucky now when Scotti needed to talk to her so badly.

Stretching up on her tiptoes and waving, Scotti yelled, "Hey, Lorna. I've got to talk to you. It's important. *Beyond* important!"

Total surprise registered on Lorna's face when she looked around. She hesitated a moment and then nodded without smiling.

Eeek! thought Scotti. She's still mad about this morning. And the worst part is, I deserve it.

Scotti had spent the morning regretting the way she had treated her best friend.

# THE GREAT DAD DISASTER

I didn't mean it. I was just upset, she reasoned. But deep down she knew that what she had done was practically unforgivable and that she owed Lorna a humongous apology.

When she got to the table, Lorna was nibbling on a grilled cheese sandwich and staring absently into space. Scotti took a deep breath and slid her tray onto the table and then sat down directly opposite her friend.

"Lorna, I know you're mad at me, and I'm sorry I was so snotty this morning," Scotti said earnestly. "Please believe me. I was just so upset at my dad. I shouldn't have taken it out on you."

Lorna flicked a glance at Scotti and put down her sandwich. "It's okay, I guess, but it really hurt. I thought you were dumping our friendship over a boy."

"Gosh, Lorna, I'd never do that. But I wouldn't have any reason to now. I told Cary I'd go out with him tonight. That's what I need to talk to you about. You've got to help me figure out what to do about my dad."

"You *what*?" cried Lorna. Her eyes were the size of dinner plates and they registered total incomprehension.

"It's okay," insisted Scotti. "Wait until I tell you what happened. I just couldn't say no because his brother Rex is going to let Cary and me cruise around in front of Rudy's for a few minutes after the movie in his red convertible. Rex will be with us, of course, to make it legal for Cary to drive, but that's okay. Everybody will see us and die of jealousy. It'll be so cool! All I need is a way to convince my father to let me go, and that's where you come in. Please, *please* help me think of a way," Scotti implored. "I don't have much time."

Lorna stared at her, unblinking, her bewildered expression gradually changing to anger.

"Did I hear you right?" she asked incredulously. "You told Cary that you *will* go out with him tonight after I broke my date with Mike so we could still be friends?"

Now it was Scotti's turn to stare. Her heart beat furiously. "You *what*?" she whispered. "Oh, Lorna, you didn't."

"I thought being your best friend was worth it," Lorna snapped. "Obviously I was wrong. Now *you're* going out with Cary, and *I'm* staying home."

She stood up abruptly, dumped the food on her tray into the garbage, and marched out of the cafeteria, leaving Scotti staring after her in shock.

Lorna raced down the hall. Her vision was blurred by tears, and she almost ran over a couple of girls in her rush to get away from the cafeteria and Scotti. The hall was crowded, and people were staring at her, but she didn't care. She had never been so angry at Scotti in her life.

"How could she *do* such a thing?" Lorna murmured as she careened around a corner, slamming into someone coming from the other direction.

She wobbled to keep from falling. "Oh, my gosh! I'm sorry!" she began, too embarrassed to look at the boy who reached out and steadied her.

"Lorna? Are you okay?"

She looked up in amazement. *"Mike!"* she cried. "Was it you I just . . . I mean."

"Hey, chill out. Everything's cool," Mike said, grinning. "No damage done. See. I still have two arms, two legs." He held up each limb and shook it out.

Lorna couldn't help laughing.

"Where were you going in such a hurry, anyway?"

"I was looking for you," Lorna announced, feeling suddenly as if fate had just stepped in and saved her from a terrible situation. She took a deep breath and went on talking before she could lose her nerve. "I just talked to my mom on the phone, and I don't have to baby-sit tonight after all. So we can go to the movie—if you still want to."

"Cool! That's totally awesome! My dad said

he'd drive us, so we'll be by for you at six-thirty, okay?''

"I'll be ready,'' said Lorna, giving him a flirty grin.

She continued on down the hall in a trance. *Yes! I am* going out with Mike tonight. And *yes!* I'll go to the mall and get a new outfit after school. I'll show Scotti.

The thought of her best friend made her feel sad again. If things had gone differently, they would be together right now, giggling over plans for their first real dates with the boys of their dreams. They might even be double dating.

Suddenly something Mike had said came back to her, and Lorna stopped in the middle of the hall.

That's it! she thought. I think I've just figured out how to get Mr. Wheeler to let Scotti go out with Cary tonight!

# 5

## FRIDAY, SEPTEMBER 17

*Dear Diary,*

*You are not going to believe everything that happened today. Dad changed his mind! I'm going out with Cary tonight! It's because of what Lorna did, but wait—I'm getting ahead of myself.*

*First, I blew up at Lorna at the bus stop because I was mad at my dad. Then I couldn't face Cary so I decided to spend the day at the mall. Then I saw Cary and his brother Rex in this gorgeous red convertible that Rex is letting Cary drive after the movie. So I lied and told Cary I could go out with him. By the time I found Lorna to ask her to help me handle*

35

*my dad, she had already broken her date with Mike to make me feel better. I felt awful.*

*Then Lorna got so mad at me that she told Mike she could go out after all, and when he said his dad would drive them, she got the idea to call her dad and ask him to drive—but get this—all four of us. He said he would, and then Lorna asked him to call my dad and explain how safe I'd be with him driving and my being with Lorna all evening. It worked! Lorna will be my best friend forever!*

*Got to go. Cary will be here any minute. More later.*

Reading over what she'd just written, Scotti smiled. My life has turned into a real-life romance novel, and I'm the star! she thought. With a flourish she grabbed her pen again and crossed out *More later.* In its place she wrote *The best is yet to come!*

She checked herself in the mirror and hurried to the living room. She didn't want to take any chances on her dad opening the door and giving Cary the third degree. If that happened, they would probably miss the first half of the movie.

# THE GREAT DAD DISASTER

"Scotti? All ready for your big date?" her father called from the family room.

"Yeah, Dad," replied Scotti.

"Come in here and let me see how you look," he said.

When Scotti entered the family room, Mr. Wheeler put down his paper, whistling low. "My, my," he said, shaking his head in wonder. "You certainly are growing up, aren't you?"

She smiled and nodded. Maybe he was having a change in attitude after all, she decided. She hoped so. She and her father had always gotten along so well.

"I know you were awfully upset with me when I turned down your first request to go out with this young man," he began thoughtfully, "but you need to understand. After all, you're the only little girl I have."

"Da-aad! I'm not a little girl," Scotti protested. It was embarrassing when he talked to her this way. And if he had had a change in attitude, it hadn't lasted very long.

"It's true, though. And I'll never forget all the special times we've had. Why, I remember taking you on the pony rides and teaching you to ride your two-wheeler. Here, look at the pictures I found," he said, whipping a handful of snapshots out of his shirt pocket and handing them to her.

"They were taken the time we went skiing in Colorado when you were three," he said proudly.

Scotti glanced at the pictures. She could actually remember that trip, even though she had been awfully small. Scotti in her snowsuit, playing in the snow. Scotti sliding down the bunny hill on tiny skis. "Yeah, Dad. These are cool."

Her father took the pictures from her outstretched hand. "You were certainly adorable. Look at those chubby red cheeks and that turned-up nose. And all those blond curls."

Thankfully the doorbell rang at that moment, sparing Scotti from any more reminiscences about her childhood.

"That must be Cary," she called over her shoulder as she rushed to open the door.

He was on the front steps, nervously fidgeting with the collar of his blue polo shirt. When he saw her, he shot her an incredible smile that made his dimple appear like magic and made her suddenly weak in the knees.

"Hi, Scotti," he said. "Are you ready?" Then looking embarrassed, he added quickly, "Of course you're ready. I can see that."

He's just as nervous as I am, she thought gratefully.

"Yeah, I'm ready," she replied. "Lorna and Mike should be here any minute. Want to wait out here?"

# THE GREAT DAD DISASTER

"Scotti!" her father's voice boomed from behind her. "Aren't you going to bring your date inside for a moment? I'd like to meet the young man who's taking out my"—he paused to clear his throat—"daughter."

"Oh . . . yeah . . . sure, Dad," she stammered, grateful that he hadn't called her his little girl. "I really meant to. I just forgot."

A look of terror crossed Cary's face, but he recovered his composure and stepped inside. "Hello, Mr. Wheeler. I'm Cary Calheim and I'm pleased to meet you."

Mr. Wheeler shook Cary's hand and said, "My pleasure. Come on in. I'd like to ask you a few questions."

"Da-*aaad!*" Scotti implored. "We don't have much time."

"This won't take long, Scotti," Mr. Wheeler said sternly. Then turning to Cary, he smiled warmly. "Nothing to be worried about, young man. I'd just like to get acquainted—find out a little bit about you."

"Yes, sir," Cary said barely above a whisper.

Scotti groaned under her breath and shot a frantic glance out the front window. If only Mr. Markham's long white Cadillac would appear magically at the front curb so that they could escape. Poor Cary. She could just die.

"So, tell me a little bit about yourself," her

father was saying. "What's this I hear about a car?"

Cary's eyebrows shot up like twin elevators, and he looked as if he were going to choke. "Car?" he managed to get out. His face was white.

Scotti froze to the spot. Did her father know about their plans for tonight?

"That's right. Scotti tells me you're rebuilding an old Mustang in your garage," said her father.

"Oh, *that* car," Cary said, visibly relieved. "That's right. It's mine and it's going to be ready by my sixteenth birthday when I get my driver's license."

Mr. Wheeler frowned. "Driver's license? Well, I just want it understood up front that my daughter will not be going out in a car driven by a teenage boy. Is that clear?"

Scotti wished she could sink through the floor and disappear forever.

Luckily the doorbell rang again.

Scotti's heart leapt for joy. "Oh, my gosh. That must be our ride!" she called out, grabbing Cary's hand and making a beeline for the door.

"Nice meeting you, Mr. Wheeler," Cary mumbled.

# THE GREAT DAD DISASTER

"Nice meeting you, too, Cary," said Scotti's father. "And, Scotti," he added.

"Yes, Dad?"

"Don't forget your ten-thirty curfew."

"Ten-thirty? But—"

Mr. Wheeler shook his head. "You've always been able to see a movie and be home by ten-thirty before," he reminded her. Then shooting a warning look at Cary, he said sharply, "I don't see why tonight should be any different just because you have a date."

Scotti didn't answer. She couldn't. Her heart was in her throat.

If tonight turns out to be a disaster, she thought, it will be all because of my dad.

# 6

----

Lorna paced back and forth in her bedroom and glanced anxiously at her watch every few seconds. Mike would be here any minute. This was it! Her big date with Mike Kilpatrick, hunk of the world and captain of the junior high cheerleading team. Half the girls in school would *kill* to be in her shoes right now.

"If only I don't do something stupid and blow it," she murmured to herself.

She could hardly wait for her parents to meet Mike, especially her dad. He had been so terrific about letting her buy a new outfit for tonight. But best of all, he had convinced Mr. Wheeler that it was okay for Scotti to go out with Cary because he would be driving them to the movie and home again.

I've probably got the most fabulous father in the world, she thought proudly.

# THE GREAT DAD DISASTER

A car door slamming at the curb made her heart jump.

"He's here!" she shouted. "Oh, my gosh. I hope I look okay." Racing to the mirror, she looked herself over for the millionth time in the past hour. The white jeans and blue and white western shirt she had gotten at the mall after school fit her to perfection. And her long dark hair had actually come out the way she'd wanted it to—for a change.

The sound of stomping on the stairway was overlaid by Tiffany's shrill voice. "Lorna! Lorna! Come on out! Your boyfriend's here!"

Lorna groaned inwardly and opened the door.

"Knock it off, Tiff!" she ordered. "He'll hear you."

Tiffany crossed her arms over her chest and stuck out a defiant lower lip. "So? He *is* here, and he *is* your boyfriend. And this is *my* house, too. I can do anything I want to, *and you can't stop me!*"

Lorna let out an exasperated breath as she hurried past Tiffany and down the stairs. When she entered the living room, Mike was sitting on the sofa, looking totally at ease, while he made conversation with her mom and dad.

"Hi, everybody," she said.

Mike's face brightened. "Hi, Lorna. Wow. You look nice."

"Thanks," she replied shyly. She wanted to tell him that he looked nice, too, but it would be too embarrassing to say something like that in front of her parents.

"Well, little darlin', come on in," said her father. "I was just having a chat with Mike, here." He chuckled. "Telling him all our family secrets."

Lorna swallowed hard. "Family secrets?" Her dad loved to joke around, and sometimes his jokes made her blush.

"Weeeell, they're not really secrets, come to think about it," Mr. Markham drawled. "For instance, there were lots of people around the time you tripped going into that Mexican restaurant and sat down in a bed of cactus. Took about a day and a half to pick out all those little stickers." He put back his head and laughed heartily.

Flames of embarrassment shot up Lorna's face. The last thing in the world she wanted Mike to know about was how clumsy she was, always bumping into door frames and things like that. After all, he was a gymnast and a cheerleader.

"Coy, I think you're embarrassing Lorna," her mother scolded gently.

"Naw," said Mr. Markham. "It's just a funny little story."

"Dad, it *isn't* funny!" Lorna said emphatically.

Her father looked at her in surprise. "Sure it is," he replied. "Besides, you were just a little tike then. Around three, if I remember."

"How old was I when Lorna sat in the cactus, Daddy?" asked Tiffany, who had just come into the room. She marched straight to the sofa and sat down beside Mike, looking him over closely while waiting for her father to answer.

"Why, sweetheart, you weren't even born yet," replied Mr. Markham, chuckling again.

"Mike, this is my little sister, Tiffany," said Lorna, adding, "sometimes known as Tiff the Terrible."

Mike seemed to be enjoying the conversation, but she was glad to change the subject, anyway.

"Hi, Tiff the Terrible," said Mike, grinning at her.

Tiffany continued to study Mike. "Is it true what Lorna said about you?" she asked.

Lorna jolted to attention, but Mike just seemed amused.

"What did Lorna say about me?" he asked good-naturedly.

"That you're a cheerleader," she piped up.

"If you are, do you wear a skirt like the girl cheer-leaders?"

*"Tiffany!"* shrieked Lorna. "Of course he doesn't wear a skirt! He's the captain of the squad, and he does terrific gymnastic routines."

"Hey, it's okay," said Mike. "She probably hasn't seen a lot of cheerleaders." Turning back to Tiffany, he said, "You see, Tiff, the guys on the squad are there mostly because of their mus-cles. You know, we let the girls stand on our shoulders, we throw them up into the air and catch them, stuff like that."

Tiffany's eyes opened wide with admiration. "Cool," she whispered.

Lorna breathed a sigh of relief. Mike was wonderful, she thought. Instead of being insulted, he had patiently explained the situation to Tiff.

"That's right, Tiffy," said her father. "I see them all the time on TV. Times sure have changed, though," he said, shaking his head. "In my time, all the cheerleaders were girls."

"I think we'd better go now, Dad," Lorna interjected. "It's time to pick up Scotti and Cary." She couldn't believe her father had said a thing like that. She wanted out of there before her dad turned the evening into a disaster.

# 7

While the boys were getting the popcorn and sodas, Scotti motioned Lorna toward the ladies' room.

As soon as the door closed behind them, Scotti bounced excitedly on her toes. "Did you see how everybody was looking at us when we got into the ticket line with Cary and Mike? Especially the girls," she said, giggling.

"Did I ever," said Lorna. "I've never had that many people looking at me at once in my entire life. Actually, though, it was Mike all the girls were staring at, not me. And did you see the way Angie Duncan was flirting with him? She'd better watch it."

"Don't worry," Scotti said dramatically. "It's fate that you've found Mike and I've found Cary. No one can come between us."

"In your dreams," scoffed Lorna. "This isn't

one of your romance novels, you know. This is real life."

"All I've got to say is, I can't believe I'm actually here with Cary, but I am—thanks to you."

Lorna smiled. "Hey, what are best friends for? I'm just glad my dad was able to talk your dad into changing his mind."

"Me, too," said Scotti, "but, believe me, that wasn't the end of the problem. My dad is *unreal*! When Cary got there, Dad cornered him and started giving him the third degree. I didn't think we'd ever get out of the house."

"*My* dad was telling Mike stories about embarrassing things I did when I was little, like the time I sat down in a cactus bed," Lorna said, rolling her eyes. "I thought I'd die!"

Scotti looked at her in surprise and then burst out laughing. "You never told me about that. That's a riot! Did you get stickers in your seat?"

"Of course," snapped Lorna. "And it took forever to get them out, but that's not the sort of thing you want your dad to tell a guy."

"You're right. I shouldn't have laughed, but you have to admit it's funny," said Scotti, laughing again. "Hey, I have something important to ask you. You know Rex is going to let Cary drive his car after the movie, right?"

Lorna nodded.

"How about you and Mike coming, too? We can wave to all our friends. It's going to be so cool. Will you come?" Scotti asked excitedly.

Lorna hesitated. "I don't know. Are you sure Cary wouldn't mind? He and Mike don't know each other very well."

"It was his idea," Scotti insisted. "Come on. Say yes. It'll be fun."

"Okay," said Lorna. "If Mike wants to."

A few minutes later Scotti was sitting beside Cary in the darkened theater. She was staring up at the screen, but instead of watching the movie, she was picturing the five of them cruising in the red convertible. Maybe Cary would even put the top down.

It's going to be awesome, she thought. *Beyond* awesome.

She glanced at Cary and felt tingly all over. He was so handsome and so much more mature than most of the boys in her grade.

I've always liked older guys, she thought, remembering the crush she'd had on Lorna's older brother Skip, who was three years older than she was.

Suddenly Cary laughed so loudly that he spilled his popcorn. All around them other kids were laughing, too. Scotti glanced at the screen.

She hadn't been paying attention, so she couldn't understand what was so funny. It just looked like a bunch of guys, standing around talking.

Taking a small sip of her soda she stole a quick sideways look at Lorna and Mike to see if they were laughing, too, and did a fast double take. They definitely were not laughing. Instead they were holding hands and whispering.

Scotti tried not to watch them, but she couldn't help it. They certainly weren't acting as if this was their first date.

They look more like a couple who's been going steady for ages, she thought, feeling a twinge of jealousy. Cary hadn't made the slightest move to hold her hand.

*Maybe now that he's with me, he doesn't like me!*

The thought flashed in Scotti's brain like a neon sign, and she shrank down in her seat in horror. Or did my dad gross him out so badly that he just wants to get through our date tonight and never ask me out again?

She glanced back at Lorna and Mike. Mike was slipping his arm around her now! Cary still had his eyes glued to the screen, laughing every couple of minutes at a zany car chase in the movie.

He doesn't even know I exist! Scotti thought.

I've got to do something to get his attention and do it fast.

Before she could lose her nerve Scotti scooted closer to Cary. "Great movie, isn't it?" she whispered loudly.

Cary gave her a big grin. "You bet. That was the funniest car chase I've ever seen. I really cracked up when those two jokers rolled that Camaro off the bridge, flipped it over in midair, and drove it right back up onto land."

"Yeah, that was great," Scotti replied half-heartedly.

"I wonder if that scene was real, or if they did it with special effects," Cary said, turning back to the movie without waiting for an answer.

Doesn't he ever think about anything but cars? she wondered, sighing in exasperation.

When the movie ended and they were filing out of the theater with the rest of the crowd, Scotti had to trail along behind Cary. He glanced back over his shoulder from time to time to make sure she was following. She couldn't help noticing that Mike and Lorna were still holding hands.

When they reached the street, Cary turned to Mike and said, "Let's look for Rex and find out where he parked the car. I can't wait to get behind the wheel."

As soon as the boys were out of earshot,

Lorna grabbed Scotti's arm. "Oh, Scotti! I'm in *love*! This is the most wonderful night of my life. Mike is so romantic!"

"That's great," Scotti said around the lump that was forming in her throat.

"I mean, all he wants to talk about is me," Lorna went on in a bubbly voice. "He wants to know *everything*! My life history. My favorite food. What kind of music I like, and all kinds of other things. I was so busy answering questions that I hardly got a chance to find out anything about him." She laughed happily. "Oh, Scotti, I never thought in my wildest dreams that my first date with Mike would be this great. Are you having as much fun with Cary?"

Scotti fought to keep tears from brimming in her eyes. She had always shared everything with Lorna. But she could never tell anyone, not even her best friend, that Cary had practically ignored her all evening. That he was a lot more interested in cars than he was in her.

She took a deep breath and plastered a fake smile on her face. "Totally," she lied. "It's fantastic. *Beyond* fantastic."

Just then Mike and Cary came racing up. Car keys jingled in Cary's hand.

"Come on, girls, it's just around the corner. Now we're really going to have some fun," he said, grabbing Scotti's hand and pulling her along the street beside him.

Scotti looked at Cary in amazement. He was actually holding her hand! It tingled inside his as she hurried along beside him.

# 8

---

Lorna's stomach was churning as she got into the backseat of the convertible with Mike. Even though it was legal for Cary to drive with Rex in the front seat between Scotti and Cary, she was nervous. What would her parents say if they found out?

In the front seat, Scotti was chattering away. Cary pushed a button and the car's top rose into the air and then folded neatly into a space behind hers and Mike's heads.

"Maybe we shouldn't do this," Lorna whispered to Mike, who already had his arm securely around her.

Mike pulled her closer. "You worry too much. Chill out, okay?"

Lorna let her head rest on Mike's shoulder. Why am I always such a chicken? she wondered.

Scotti tries everything. Why can't I be more like her?

Suddenly the car roared to life.

"Hey, everybody, here we go!" Scotti yelled from the front seat. Her words were almost blown away in the rush of wind as the car sprang forward and careened around a corner.

Scotti twisted around in her seat so that she was facing Mike and Lorna. She had to hold her hair down to keep it from blowing into her face. "Rex is going to duck out of sight when we go past Rudy's. Get ready to wave."

This will be fun after all, Lorna thought. She tried to push away from Mike and sit up straight.

"Hey, where're you going?" said Mike, pulling her back again.

"To wave, silly. To see and be seen. Come on, Mike. This will be fun," Lorna urged and tugged on his arm.

He let her pull him forward. "Okay. One wave," he said. He raised a hand and waved briefly. Then he sank back in the seat again, grinning at her. "How's that?"

"Mi-*ike*," she said. "Nobody saw you. We haven't even gotten to Rudy's yet. Come on. Wave with me when we get there. Please?" She dragged out the word "please" and gave him her best pleading look.

He shrugged. "Okay, if it'll make you happy," he said, pushing himself back up to the edge of the seat. "I'll wave my arm off."

Feathery little thrills raced up her back. Mike was wonderful. He was romantic, and gorgeous, and everything she wanted in a boyfriend.

*I'm in love! I'm in love!* she wanted to shout.

They were coming up on Rudy's now. It was a typical Friday night, and there were almost as many people standing around outside as there usually were crowded inside. Lorna felt like a movie star, sitting in the backseat of the red convertible with Mike Kilpatrick beside her.

This is cool, she thought happily. Or as Scotti would put it, *beyond* cool.

In the front seat, Scotti was having the time of her life. Cary had held her hand all the way to the car, and he had been talking up a storm to her ever since, even though Rex was between them. Of course it had been car talk. He'd explained to her that Rex's car wasn't just any ordinary car. He said it had dual carbs and chrome headers—whatever they were—but at least he had been talking to her.

And now, as they approached Rudy's, Rex

scooted down in the seat, out of sight. The kids in front were beginning to notice the gorgeous red convertible cruising past. She saw Erin Mooney and Jamie Spacek gasp in surprise and point at them. Other heads turned to look. Scotti thought she would burst with excitement.

She leaned out of the car and waved as hard as she could. "Hi, everybody! Hi, Brianna! Hi, Sean! Hi, Missy!" She was out of breath when she turned to Cary and said, "Wow, was that *fun*! But it was over so *fast*! I didn't get to say hi to half the kids I knew. Can we go by again?"

Cary's left arm rested on top of the door frame, and he was driving with the other one. She knew he was trying to look cool.

"Sure," he said. "We've got lots of time. Right, Rex?"

"Sure, as long as I can sit up when we're not going past Rudy's," he said and chuckled.

When Cary turned the corner to go around the block, Scotti glanced at her watch. It was going on ten. If they cruised for half an hour, then called Mr. Markham to come get them, it would be after eleven when she got home. Her dad had been definite about her being home by ten-thirty. But surely he would understand that things were different when you were on a date. And besides, he trusted Mr. Markham to make sure everything was okay.

Scotti felt her excitement swell again as Rudy's came back into sight and Rex ducked again.

"Hey, look!" she heard one boy shout. "Here comes Calheim again!"

This time everyone was lined up, waiting for them and watching as they drove past.

"Slow down," urged Scotti.

Laughing happily, she waved both hands and shouted to her friends. Beside her, Cary was waving, too. It was obvious that everyone was impressed.

"Looking good!" shouted one boy, who leaned toward them and raised his thumb in a victory sign.

"Way to go!" called out someone else.

Scotti heard a whistle from someone in the crowd.

She was glowing with pride. Cary was a terrific driver. He stayed under the speed limit and stopped at all the stop signs. Even her dad would have trouble finding anything to criticize *if* he could see Cary driving right now.

But it went too fast again, and Scotti turned all the way around in her seat and kept waving after they had gone by.

"Lorna! Mike! Isn't this fun?" she shouted, glancing toward them.

But to Scotti's amazement, they weren't paying the least bit of attention. Her mouth dropped open. They were snuggled in one corner of the backseat—kissing.

# 9

Scotti had a funny feeling in the pit of her stomach for the rest of the evening. It was fun driving past Rudy's and waving to her friends, but she couldn't get the sight of Lorna and Mike kissing out of her mind.

That just isn't like Lorna, she thought. She's only had one other date, and that was with nerdy Fletcher Holloway. It had been a total disaster. But Scotti knew down deep that her real problem with Mike and Lorna's kissing was jealousy.

Mike liked Lorna. Cary liked cars. Even with the four of them wedged into the backseat of the Markhams' car for the drive home, Cary hadn't put his arm around her. And she suspected that the only reason he had held her hand when they raced to Rex's car was to make her hurry. She was positive that tonight would be their one and only date.

"Thanks, Mr. Markham, and good night, everybody," she said when the big white Cadillac pulled up in front of her house and she got out.

Cary had gotten out, too, and to Scotti's surprise he leaned in and said, "That goes for me, too, Mr. Markham. Thanks for the ride. I can walk the rest of the way."

A light glared over the front door, and Scotti stayed in the shadows near the curb. "I had a really nice time tonight, Cary," she said softly. "Thanks for everything."

"Yeah, I had fun, too," Cary replied. He shifted his weight from one foot to the other and looked away.

Scotti bit her lip nervously. Why didn't he say something else? Was he trying to figure out how to tell her good-bye—forever?

"I was wondering if . . ." he began slowly and stopped.

He shifted his weight back again and looked at her. It was too dark for her to see if he was smiling. She held her breath.

"Would you go out with me again?" he asked just above a whisper. "Maybe next Friday?"

Scotti wanted to jump up and down and shout. But she caught herself and said instead,

"Sure, Cary. I'd love to." It surprised her how cool she sounded.

"Terrific," he said, and the word came out in a rush of breath as if he hadn't believed she'd say yes. "Maybe Mike and Lorna will want to go, too."

"Sure. We'll ask them."

Scotti's heart was beating wildly. She knew she should say good night and go inside, but her feet were glued to the sidewalk. *He does like me, after all!* she thought deliriously.

Cary didn't make a move to leave, and Scotti was racking her brain so hard for something to talk about that she was suddenly aware that he had moved closer to her.

*He's going to kiss me!*

He looked into her eyes and moved closer again. She turned her face up to his.

When their lips were almost touching, the front door opened.

"Scotti! Is that you?"

She jumped a foot, and Cary leapt back quickly. She sighed. "Yes, Dad. It's me. I'll be there in a minute."

"Um . . . I'd better go," Cary mumbled and started to walk away.

"Just a minute, young man," boomed her father. He had come out of the house and was walking down the front steps. Mr. Wheeler shaded his eyes from the bright light over the door and peered into the darkness. "I want both of you here *this instant.*"

Oh, no, Scotti thought as they marched obediently toward her father. Her heart was in her throat.

"Where have you been, and why are you so late?" he demanded.

"But, Dad," Scotti began. "We went to the movie. You knew that was where we were going, and Mr. Markham just brought us home."

Mr. Wheeler drew his eyebrows together in a frown. "The movie has been over for more than an hour."

"Then we went to Rudy's. You know Lorna and I always go to Rudy's after the movie," Scotti argued.

She knew her voice was high and squeaky. She sounded like a little girl begging to get out of being sent to her room, but she couldn't help it. She had never been so embarrassed in her life. And what did Cary think?

"That's right, sir, we went to Rudy's," Cary volunteered in a shaky voice.

Mr. Wheeler glared at Cary and then turned to Scotti. "When you weren't home at ten-thirty, I called Rudy's. They said you weren't there."

"But we *were* . . . I mean, it was

crowded," Scotti sputtered. "They probably just couldn't see us."

"We were outside part of the time, standing around and talking to some friends," said Cary. "I'm sorry if you were worried."

"Well, I suppose they might not know if you were outside," Mr. Wheeler said after a moment.

"I guess I'd better go in now," said Scotti. She turned to Cary and tried as hard as she could to say thank you with her eyes.

Cary looked relieved, too. "Sure," he said. "Good night, Scotti. Good night, Mr. Wheeler." In an instant he had disappeared down the dark street.

Scotti followed her father into the house. Her face was burning with humiliation.

"Dad, how could you say that in front of Cary?" she implored. "Don't you know how it made me feel?"

Her father heaved a deep sigh and put an arm around her. "Sweetheart," he began, "if I don't protect my little girl, who will? Don't think I don't know what boys are after."

Scotti rolled her eyes and shrugged off his arm. "Dad, Cary's not like that. Believe me. He's really nice. And I'm not a little girl anymore."

He shook his head solemnly. "I know you don't want to believe this, but boys *are* all alike. They're after one thing. You'll find that out sooner or later. I know. Believe it or not, I used to be one," he said and chuckled at his own joke. Then his face turned serious again. "That's why I set rules. If you're out on a date, I want to know where you're going. I also want you to be home no later than ten-thirty from now on. Any later than that and you're grounded. Do I make myself clear?"

"But, Da-*aaad*! That's so unfair!"

"Nevertheless, those are the rules," he said sternly.

Scotti marched to her room and slammed the door. Tears were streaming down her face as she unlocked her diary and wrote furiously. Running out of space on the page, she wrote up one side margin and down the other, venting her anger and humiliation. Finally, in the last tiny space on the page, she wrote:

> *I have the most suspicious and the most overprotective father in the world!!!! Lorna is so lucky. She has a perfect boyfriend and a perfect father. I'm so jealous I could die!*

Lorna was looking out her bedroom window, gazing toward the Wheelers' house, when she saw Scotti's light go out.

Darn, she thought. If only I had called her

before she went to bed. I need to talk to her about Mike.

She crawled into bed and turned out her own light, thinking about her evening with Mike. It had been fabulous—mostly. He was the most wonderful boy she had ever known, and he liked *her*! It was almost impossible to believe that someone so handsome and popular could possibly like her, of all people.

There are lots of prettier girls, she reasoned. And lots with better personalities. What could he possibly see in me?

She tossed and turned, unable to go to sleep.

Everything was perfect except for one thing, she thought. Mike was wonderfully romantic, but he was coming on too fast, and she wasn't sure how to stop him. Maybe Scotti could help.

# 10

---

**L**orna awoke with a start the next morning when Tiffany burst into her room and leapt onto her bed.

"Wake up, Lorna," she said. "Guess what?"

Scowling, Lorna opened one eye. "I give up. What?"

"Mommy and Daddy said we're going to The Leaning Tower of Pizza for lunch and to a movie afterward. Wanna come? Say yes."

Lorna struggled into a sitting position. "Pizza. Yum. I'd love to, Tiff, but Scotti and I are going to the football game this afternoon."

"The movie will be better," Tiff said in a pouty voice. "Go with us. Please?"

Lorna gave her little sister a hug, thinking that Tiff could be really bratty sometimes, but down deep she was a pretty sweet kid.

"I have to go to the ball game. It's the first

game of the season for Colleyville Junior High, and besides, Mike's cheering today. I promised him I'd be there."

Tiffany wriggled out of the hug and climbed down from the bed, placing her fists firmly on her hips. "Boyfriends, *yuck!*" she said, and stomped out of the room.

Lorna sighed and slipped down under the covers again. She lay there for a while daydreaming about their date last night. Mike was so sweet. And so caring.

So what if he got a little carried away for a first date? she thought. That doesn't mean he'll always be that way. I was probably worried for nothing. And besides, I really do like kissing him.

By the time Scotti came by after lunch to go to the game she had completely convinced herself that everything was going to be cool with Mike. Nothing she couldn't handle.

"Mom will be home from New York this afternoon," said Scotti as they walked along in the warm afternoon sunshine on their way to the stadium. "Boy, I can't wait. Dad is driving me berserk. You won't believe what he did last night."

"What now?" Lorna asked sympathetically.

"As soon as you guys drove away, Dad came storming out of the house demanding to know where we had been and why we were so late. I almost died on the spot," Scotti said dramatically. "And get this—when I wasn't home by ten-thirty, Dad called Rudy's checking up on me."

"We weren't at Rudy's. We were in Rex's car," Lorna said with alarm. "He didn't find out about that, did he?"

"No, but there's more," said Scotti. She went on to describe the rest of the scene with her father.

"I guess I'm luckier than I realize," Lorna said. "My dad gives me a lot of freedom when it comes to curfews. He keeps telling me that he knows I'm responsible enough to know when to come home."

They walked along in silence for a few minutes. Lorna hoped she hadn't said the wrong thing and made Scotti feel worse than ever about her own father. She hadn't meant to.

But at the same time, Scotti seems to be getting her feelings hurt a lot lately, thought Lorna, and I don't understand why.

The stadium was already getting crowded by the time the girls got there, but Lorna spotted Brianna Chambers and Missy Walker waving to them and pointing to empty seats in the row behind them.

"Come on," said Lorna, taking the steps

three at a time. "Brianna and Missy are holding seats for us."

Before Lorna and Scotti could get settled in their seats, Brianna said in a loud voice, "We saw you guys and your big dates last night. Pret-ty im-pres-sive, if you ask me. Right, Missy?"

"Totally," said Missy. "Hey, Lorna. Give me some pointers. I'd like to land a hunk like Mike Kilpatrick myself. We were sitting right behind you during the movie, and you guys were pretty steamy."

Lorna knew she was turning purple. "We met in math class and sort of got acquainted," she said, trying not to let them see how flustered she was. "We just hit it off right, I guess," she added with a shrug.

"You hit it off, all right," said Brianna. "Whoa!"

Lorna kept hoping that Scotti would jump in and say something clever to get her off the hook the way she usually did when Lorna got herself into a sticky situation, but Scotti didn't say a word. Scotti seemed to be ignoring the whole conversation, gazing around the crowd as if she were trying to spot someone.

She's more interested in looking for Cary than helping out her best friend, Lorna thought angrily.

# THE GREAT DAD DISASTER

Suddenly the school band struck up the fight song and a roar broke out in the stadium as the crowd rose to its feet. Lorna stood up, too. The football team was trotting onto the field led by eight cheerleaders, five girls, and three boys. Mike was in the lead, doing an amazing tumbling run filled with double and triple flips.

Lorna sucked in her breath in awe and forgot all about Brianna's and Missy's remarks.

Scotti felt as if everyone in the world was against her. She could hardly talk to her best friend anymore. Her mother was away from home when Scotti needed her most. Her father's strictness was threatening to ruin her life. And then there was Cary. She couldn't spot him anywhere in the entire stadium.

He's probably home working on his car! she thought angrily.

When the rest of the crowd stood up to cheer the team onto the field, Scotti stayed seated. She felt abandoned. Everybody came to the school's games. Absolutely *everybody*. Except Cary.

Maybe he's gone to the library to read *Popular Mechanics*!

She felt a nudge on her arm.

"Aren't you going to yell?" Lorna asked,

71

sounding annoyed. "Come on. Stand up and look at Mike. He's *awesome!*"

Scotti stood up, but she didn't look at the field or at Mike.

"I think I'll go to the refreshment stand," she said.

She started to ask Lorna if she wanted anything and changed her mind. She could sense Lorna's hurt expression as she made her way across the row and down the steps, but she couldn't turn around and go back.

Why should I? she thought. Lorna has everything. She has a dad who understands how grown-up she is and a boyfriend who cares about her and not cars. She doesn't need me.

# 11

Scotti was scuffing across the grass toward the refreshment stand when she heard her name.

"Hey, Scotti! Wait up!"

To her astonishment Cary was hurrying through the front gate and straight toward her.

"Am I late? Has the game started?" he asked breathlessly. "I was working on my car, and I forgot to look at my watch," he added apologetically.

Scotti didn't know whether to laugh or get angry all over again. He had made it to the game, but he was late. And he was obviously glad to see her, but he had spent most of the day with his car.

She was glad to see him, too. She smiled and said, "The game's just starting."

"Great. Let's find some seats—unless you're already sitting with somebody," he said.

Scotti glanced up at Lorna high in the stands. They had been packed into the row so tightly that there had barely been room for the two of them. There was no use trying to squeeze Cary in. There was no way to get Lorna's attention, either, to let her know she'd be sitting with Cary.

Oh, well, she thought. I'll talk to her later.

"I was sitting with Lorna, Brianna, and Missy, but I'm sure they won't get jealous if I sit with you," she said.

"They'd better not," he said, grinning.

It took a while, but they finally found seats near the end zone. Scotti kept glancing up at Lorna, trying to get her attention, but Lorna never looked her way.

I guess I'll just have to call her when I get home, Scotti thought, midway through the third quarter.

"Okay if I walk you home?" Cary asked as they filed out of the stadium after the game.

"Sure," Scotti answered happily.

"Did I ever tell you how I got my car?" Cary asked as they walked along.

Scotti looked at him in astonishment. She had just about had it with that car. When he wasn't working on it, he was talking about it.

If Cary noticed her silence, he didn't let on.

"I started saving the money I earned cutting lawns when I was twelve," he said. "By the time I was fourteen I had enough to buy it. Boy, it was an old junker then. But my dad said that if I did good work fixing it up, I'd have a great car when I was finished. A classic."

"Really?" she said, trying to sound interested.

"Dad's bought most of the parts, and I'm paying him back as fast as I can."

"I suppose you want to be a racing car driver someday," Scotti said. "I mean, you love cars so much."

Cary shook his head. "Don't laugh," he said sheepishly, "but I've wanted to be a veterinarian ever since I was a little kid and saw my dog Goofy get hit by a car. That little dog was in so much pain, and I couldn't do anything about it. He died before we could get him to the vet. It was awful, and I made up my mind then that since I couldn't help Goofy, I'd help other animals."

At first Scotti didn't know what to say. She had been wrong about Cary. He wasn't just a car freak. He was working hard for something he wanted, and he was a tender and caring person.

She reached out and touched his arm. "I wouldn't laugh about a thing like that. It's really sweet, and I think you'll make a great veterinarian."

"So, do you have big plans for your future?" he asked.

"I'm going to be a writer," Scotti announced proudly.

"A writer? Wow," said Cary. "I'm impressed. What are you going to write?"

Scotti smiled. "Now don't you laugh. I've already written two novels."

He gave her a skeptical look. "Two novels? What are they about?"

Scotti gulped. How could she tell him that they were romance novels, starring herself and Skip Markham, Lorna's older brother, whom she used to have a humongous crush on?

"They're just fiction," she said quickly. "You know, stories I made up."

"Can I read one sometime?" he asked.

Eeek! she thought. Recovering quickly, she said, "Maybe someday, if I can still find them."

Cary was thoughtful for a moment and then said, "Do you know one of the things I like about you, Scotti?"

"No," she said in surprise.

"I really appreciate how you seem interested in my car. I know it must get pretty boring sometimes when I talk about it so much. But most girls don't care anything about what boys are interested in. All they care about is how they look. And the latest gossip. I'm glad you're different."

Scotti was stunned. All this time she'd been hating his car, and he'd been thinking she liked it. But there was more to what he said than that. He was giving her a real compliment. He was saying she was a special person.

"Thanks, Cary," she said shyly. "I like you, too . . . a lot."

As soon as they turned the corner onto her street, she could see her father in the front yard raking leaves. He hadn't noticed them yet.

"I don't think your dad likes me very much," Cary said.

"His problem is he thinks all boys are monsters," said Scotti. "He just needs to get to know you better."

"I'm not sure I have the nerve to let him get to know me in person," said Cary. "Maybe I should make a videotape about my life and send it to him."

Scotti laughed. "That would be funny. But seriously, he gets a little weird sometimes, but he's pretty nice most of the time. We have some terrific times together."

Just then Mr. Wheeler looked up from his

raking. He scowled when he saw Scotti and Cary coming toward him.

"See, what did I tell you. He hates me," Cary whispered out of the side of his mouth.

"It's okay," Scotti whispered back. "Just act friendly."

"Well, what are you two doing together again so soon?" her dad asked in a grumpy voice.

"Um . . . Hi, Mr. Wheeler. We're just walking home from the ball game," Cary said nervously. "I only live four blocks from here. Over on Rolling Hills Road." Turning to Scotti, he added, "I'd better go now. I'll see you at school Monday."

"Sure. See you," she replied.

"Bye, Mr. Wheeler," Cary called over his shoulder as he trotted down the street.

"Scotti, I thought you went to the ball game with Lorna," said her father.

"I did, Dad. Why are you being so suspicious of Cary? All we did was walk home in broad daylight."

"Sweetheart," her father began, his voice softening, "I just don't like to see you spending too much time with Cary. You were just together last night, you know."

"But, Dad, you don't understand. He's really nice."

# THE GREAT DAD DISASTER

"That's not the point," said her father. "Spending too much time with a boy can lead to trouble. I don't want you to see Cary more than once a week, and that's final."

Scotti threw up her hands in disgust and stomped into the house. When she reached her room, she took off her jacket and angrily pitched it toward the bed. She blinked in surprise when she saw that it had landed next to a box wrapped in gold foil.

"A present!" she cried, grabbing the box and tearing off the wrapping. Her eyes widened in delight when she saw that it was candy. "Turtles! My absolute favorite."

As she was fumbling with the box, an envelope fluttered to the floor. She opened it and read the message inside.

*Dear Scotti,*
*This is just a little peace offering. Hope you can forgive your old dad for blowing his top last night.*
*I love you,*
*Dad*

Scotti sat down on the edge of the bed and traced the picture of the chocolate candy on the box lid with the tip of her finger. She knew why he had chosen Turtles. She and her dad ate Turtles when Mrs. Wheeler was flying. It was their special secret. Their own private joke.

This is so confusing, she thought. First Dad apologizes for coming unglued last night, and then he does the same thing all over again when I show up with Cary.

Sighing, she put the candy on her desk. Mom will be home in just a few hours, she reminded herself. If I can last that long.

# 12

Lorna felt a stab of jealousy as she watched Mike toss Holly Hooper into the air and catch her again. Holly was the cutest cheerleader on the squad, and she was tiny and probably as light as a feather. She had been flirting with Mike all through the game, and Lorna was furious. Actually, all the cheerleaders had been flirting with Mike. She could certainly understand why. He was the best-looking guy on the squad and the most athletic.

And he's all mine, she thought with satisfaction.

She felt a tap on her shoulder.

"What happened to Scotti?" Brianna asked.

Lorna frowned. "I don't know. She said she was going to the refreshment stand, but that was ages ago. I've been watching for her but I haven't seen her."

"Maybe we should go look for her," suggested Missy.

"She couldn't get lost," said Lorna. "Maybe she found someone else she'd rather sit with."

"Yeah, like Cary," Brianna said, grinning. "Hey, I think I see them. Isn't that them down by the end zone?"

Lorna looked where Brianna was pointing. Scotti and Cary were in the second row, almost at the end of the bleachers.

Thanks a lot, best friend, Lorna thought. Just go off with someone else and don't tell me.

She turned back to the game. Colleyville had just scored a touchdown, and the cheerleaders were racing onto the field. While the others led the victory cheer, Mike was performing incredible acrobatics, flipping forward and backward and forward again.

Lorna caught her breath as she watched. All thoughts of Scotti were gone from her mind.

Mike was waiting for her beside the ticket booth after the game. As she hurried toward him, she was aware that almost every girl who went past him either smiled or waved or said something to him.

"Great game, wasn't it?" he said excitedly. "I never thought we could win by two touchdowns."

"That wasn't the only thing that was great," said Lorna. "You were terrific. You should try out for the Olympics."

Mike slipped an arm around her as they headed out the gate. "It just takes practice," he said modestly. "There's going to be a victory celebration at Rudy's. Want to go?"

Lorna started to say yes and stopped herself. All the girls who had flirted with Mike at the game would probably be at Rudy's, too. The last thing she wanted was to have to compete for his attention with someone like Holly Hooper.

"Why don't we go to my house and make a pizza. We've got all the stuff."

"Sounds good to me," said Mike.

When they got to the Markham house, Mike followed her in and stopped, looking around and cocking his head as if he were listening for something. "Are we alone?" he asked, his eyes brightening.

"Sure. My parents took Tiffy to a movie, and Skip probably went off with his friends for the afternoon," she said, and suddenly regretted it.

Mike was moving toward her, a dreamy look in his eyes.

"Forget about making pizza for now," he said, scooping her into his arms and kissing her.

Alarms were going off in her head as she

pushed him away. "It's after four. My parents will be home any minute."

He reached for her again. "Then we'd better take advantage of the time we have, hadn't we?"

"I don't think we should, Mike. I mean—"

He kissed her again. "What's the matter? We like each other, don't we?"

"Of course we do, but what if my parents walked in?" she insisted.

"Let me worry about that," said Mike, sitting down on the sofa. "Come on. We'll listen for their car."

Lorna's heart was racing. She wished they had gone to Rudy's. She even wished her parents would come home. Right now. Before things got out of hand. Mike was pushing things too fast, and it was scary.

"Come on," Mike urged. "What are you waiting for?"

"I think I hear the car," she lied. "Come on, let's pretend we're making pizza!" She raced for the kitchen.

She knew he had followed her into the room and was leaning against the door frame watching her dash around, getting out the pan, a can of refrigerated pizza dough, and a jar of sauce and dumping them all on the counter.

"What kind of pizza do you like? We've got

pepperoni, and three kinds of cheese, and mush-
rooms, and probably even a can of anchovies because my brother Skip loves anchovies,
and . . ." She stopped, out of breath, and
looked at Mike. She knew she had been chattering, but it was because he made her so nervous.

He was grinning at her. "Okay, so now
you've got all the stuff out, and your parents will
think we're making a pizza. So now come back
in here with me, and we'll listen for that car
you imagined you heard a couple of minutes
ago."

She stared at him, not knowing exactly what
to say or do. What if she refused, and he got
mad? What if he got so mad that he never asked
her out again? There were plenty of other girls
who would go out with him. Like the entire
cheerleading squad! And she really did want to
kiss him. But—

Suddenly the door to the garage flew open,
and Tiffany bounded into the room.

"Hi, Lorna. Hi, Mike. Guess what? I just saw
*Aladdin!*"

Her parents followed Tiffany into the room.
Lorna almost collapsed. She hadn't heard the
car, and obviously Mike hadn't either. What if she
had gone into the living room with Mike and her

parents had walked in on them? She could feel her face flaming.

"Well, hello there, Mike," said her father. He strode across the room and pumped Mike's hand. "Glad to see you kids here at the house enjoying yourselves."

Lorna grinned sheepishly and darted a quick look at Mike. He looked totally cool and composed, as usual.

Her mother chuckled softly and handed Lorna a large flat box with The Leaning Tower of Pizza printed on the top. "There's really no need to make pizza. Tiffy was too excited about the movie to eat much of hers, and we brought it home. All you have to do is reheat it."

"Oh, boy, a doggie bag," said Mike, laughing. "Believe me, we'll take it. The Leaning Tower of Pizza makes the best in town."

Mr. Markham put a fatherly arm around Mike and said, "Son, I like you a lot. You're a fine young man. Why don't you come home with Lorna after school and do your homework together sometimes. I know she gets lonely here by herself with her mother and me working, Tiffy at her little friend's house down the street, and Skip at his after-school job."

A slow smile spread over Mike's face. "Gosh, that's a great idea, Mr. Markham. I could sure use some help with the math, and Lorna's good at that.''

"Well, you can just consider it a permanent invitation,'' he said in his soft Texas drawl.

Lorna felt her heart sink to the pit of her stomach as she pictured herself alone with Mike every day after school.

Dad doesn't know what he's done! she thought. *Now what am I going to do?*

# 13

_____

"**M**om, you've got to do something about Dad!" Scotti pleaded. "He's ruining my life!"

Her mother had been home exactly five minutes, and Scotti had followed her into the bedroom where she was unpacking her suitcase.

An amused smile crossed Helene Wheeler's face. "I've only been gone three days, and already your father has ruined your life? What on earth has he done that's so terrible?"

"Mom, this is serious. He thinks Cary Calheim's going to rape me."

Mrs. Wheeler dropped the blouse she had been shaking out and looked at Scotti in alarm. "What! Isn't that the boy you went out with last night? What happened?"

Scotti nodded and started at the beginning, explaining as patiently as she could what had happened.

# THE GREAT DAD DISASTER

"Mom, Cary's just not like that. He's kind. And sweet. And he loves animals. He even wants to be a *veterinarian*! I can't understand why Dad won't at least give him a chance," Scotti lamented. "He doesn't even want me to be with Cary. I can't see him more than once a week. *It isn't fair!*"

Her mother smiled sympathetically. "Sweetheart, I'm sorry you're so upset with your father. I know it seems unfair, but he's only trying to protect you."

"And another thing, Mom, he keeps calling me his *little girl*. I'm not a little girl anymore. I'm getting older every day."

"Of course you are, Scotti," said her mother. "And now that I've heard your side, I promise I'll have a talk with him. How's that?"

"Thanks, Mom . . . and, Mom, will you do it right away? I won't be able to stand it if I have to wait a whole week to see Cary again."

Scotti was feeling a little better when she left her mother to finish unpacking and went back to her own room. There was still one problem nagging at her, though. Lorna.

Why is it so hard to talk to her these days? Scotti wondered. She stared into space and thought about how their relationship seemed to be changing.

*I* still want to be best friends, Scotti assured herself. It's just that Lorna has gotten so carried away over Mike that she's forgotten I even exist. I can't let things stay this way.

Sighing, she picked up the phone and punched in Lorna's number.

Lorna had been sitting at her desk staring at the phone. She really needed to talk to someone about her problem with Mike, but it wasn't the sort of thing she could share with just anyone. It was too personal. Too secret. It was the kind of thing only a best friend could help with.

But Scotti has been acting strange the last few days, she thought and frowned. Distant. As if she has other, *more important* things on her mind. Cary, of course.

"Well, I'm not going to call her first," Lorna said aloud. "If she wants to talk to me, let her call."

At that same instant the phone rang.

"Hello?"

"Hi, Lorna. It's me, Scotti."

"Oh, hi, Scotti," Lorna said in surprise.

"I hope you aren't mad that I didn't come back up and sit with you at the game today," Scotti said quickly. "I met Cary by the refreshment stand. I knew there wasn't enough room for him up where we were sitting, so we found another spot. I tried to get your attention, but I couldn't. I guess I should have come back up and told you."

"That's okay," said Lorna, feeling relieved. "Brianna saw where you were sitting. I . . . I wasn't mad, not really."

"I wouldn't blame you if you were," said Scotti. "I'm really sorry."

"Do you think you could come over?" Lorna asked. "I really need to talk to you about something."

"Sure. I'll be right there. I've got something to talk to you about, too," said Scotti.

Lorna hung up, feeling better already.

When Scotti reached Lorna's room a few minutes later, Lorna started talking before the door closed.

"I've got a real problem with Mike, and Dad's making it worse," Lorna began.

Scotti looked at her in astonishment. "And *I've* got a real problem with Cary, and it's all because of *my* dad."

As they had so many times before, they sat cross-legged on Lorna's water bed and told each other their problems.

When each had finished her story, Lorna

shook her head and said, "This is unbelievable. Remember last year when we thought we had the wrong moms? Well, I definitely think we have the wrong dads."

Scotti nodded. "I agree. Maybe we were switched at birth. I could certainly use a dad who is more trusting and lenient, and you could use one who's more protective."

"Yeah, but what are we going to do about it?" asked Lorna, grinning. "I don't think either of our parents would go for letting us switch again."

"Mom just got home a little while ago, and I talked to her about Dad," said Scotti. "She said she'd talk to him, but I doubt if it will do much good. He's pretty stubborn, especially when it comes to protecting *his little girl,*" she added sarcastically. "Why don't you talk to your mom?"

"Are you kidding?" cried Lorna. "You know me better than that. I could never talk to her about *that*! I mean, what would she think? I'd be so embarrassed I'd die."

"I do know how shy you are and how easily you get embarrassed, but she's your mother," Scotti insisted.

Lorna shook her head. "I just couldn't."

"Okay, let's go to plan B," said Scotti. "I've just had a brilliant idea. *Beyond* brilliant. Since

# THE GREAT DAD DISASTER

I'm probably going to have to sneak around to see Cary during the week, and since you don't dare be alone with Mike, what if Cary and I just happen to drop by after school on Monday?"

"Scotti, you're a genius!" cried Lorna.

I *am* a genius, Scotti thought happily. It's a perfect plan. What could possibly go wrong?

# 14

Lorna was at the kitchen table, playing Chutes and Ladders with Tiffany the next afternoon when Scotti called.

"Didn't I tell you what would happen?" Scotti began in a huff. "Mom talked to Dad, but did he give in? Of course not. What's worse, he even convinced *her*!" Scotti was practically shouting into the phone.

"Calm down," urged Lorna. "Start at the beginning."

"Okay, you know I told you yesterday that Mom was going to talk to him."

"Right," said Lorna.

"Well, I felt really hopeful when he left for work this morning. He was in a great mood, and we went through our usual good-bye routine that we do when he's going to be flying for three days. He told me to keep my flaps up, and I told him

94

happy landing. Airplane stuff. Anyway, as soon as he left, I went to Mom and asked her if she'd talked to him. That was when she dropped the bomb.''

"So what did she say?'' Lorna asked when Scotti paused.

"She said that she agreed with Dad. Can you believe that? She said that since I had only known Cary a couple of weeks, and since they didn't really know much about him or his family, I should cool it and only see him once a week. Blah, blah, blah. She talked for fifteen minutes about how they were only trying to do what was right, and how I shouldn't neglect my friends and my schoolwork because of a boy.''

"Gosh, Scotti, I'm sorry,'' said Lorna. "I thought your mother would understand.''

"So did I,'' said Scotti. "But Dad really did a snow job. She said he's probably remembering what it was like to be a teenage boy, and that's why he's so protective. I told her he's *over*protective. They want to keep me a baby forever. What bothers me is that neither of them gives *me* any credit. I can handle things.''

Lorna wanted to tell Scotti that handling guys wasn't as easy as she thought it would be, but she didn't. Instead, she said, "Want to come over and play Chutes and Ladders with Tiffy and me? It's something to do, and it's raining so we can't ride our bikes."

"Thanks, but I think I'll just go drink poison," Scotti replied.

Lorna laughed. She knew Scotti was only kidding, but she couldn't hang up without trying to cheer her up.

"You and Cary are still coming over after school tomorrow, aren't you?"

"I haven't talked to Cary about it yet, but I'm sure he'll say yes," Scotti assured her. "I'll just have to make sure my parents don't see us sneaking into your house."

"Come on, Lorna. It's your turn," Tiffany called.

"Tiff the Terrible's calling. Gotta go," Lorna said to Scotti. "See you tomorrow morning at the bus stop."

When Lorna went to bed later that night, she closed her eyes and thought about Mike. A shiver of happiness ran through her. It wasn't just because he was so handsome, and so popular, and so athletic. It was more than that. He had a way of making her feel so special. With Scotti's and Cary's help she wouldn't have to worry about losing him before she figured out how to slow him down.

. . .

# THE GREAT DAD DISASTER

Scotti knew that sneaking around behind her parents' backs to see Cary was wrong. But they're wrong about Cary, and they're wrong about me, too! she thought stubbornly as she dressed for school the next morning.

As soon as the bus pulled up in front of Colleyville Junior High, she headed up the street toward the place where Cary had pulled up in his brother's red convertible on Friday.

She hurried along, thinking about how much fun it was going to be for the four of them to do their homework together at Lorna's house. No snoopy parents looking over their shoulders. Listening in on their conversation. Acting suspicious. And as pleased as she was that her idea would help Lorna, she couldn't wait to be with Cary.

As she scanned the traffic, the red convertible turned the corner at the light and eased into a parking place at the curb. Rex was in the passenger seat beside him.

"Hey, Scotti. Did you come to meet me?" Cary asked, climbing out of the car. He sounded pleased, and his smile was so big the dimple in his chin was the size of a crater.

"Sure. I thought you might get lonesome walking all the way to school by yourself," she said, giving him a fast grin.

"Cool," he said, slipping her hand inside his.

"There's another reason I came," she said. "There's something I want to ask you. Mike is going over to Lorna's after school so they can do homework together. She asked if we'd come, too. Doesn't that sound like fun?"

"Sure, but you know that I work on my car every afternoon after school," he said soberly.

Scotti's heart sank. "Do you have to work on it *every* day?"

"No, I don't have to work on it *every* day, but . . ." He paused and looked at her apologetically. "The last part I need is coming in today. Dad's taking off early from work to pick it up for me, and we're going to start putting it in. When we get that done, my car will finally be finished."

"Oh, that's great," said Scotti, trying to keep the disappointment out of her voice. She could see the pride shining in his eyes.

"I'm sorry, Scotti," said Cary. "It's just that . . ."

"I understand," she said, thinking that she really did understand. His car was the most important thing in his life.

But she would worry about that later. Right now she was worried about what she was going to tell Lorna.

# 15

As Lorna and Mike walked along after school, she knew that each step was taking her closer to one of the biggest challenges of her life, and she wasn't prepared.

"You're awfully quiet," said Mike. "Something wrong?"

"Gosh, no," she said in a squeaky, nervous voice. "Everything's great."

Her mouth was dry, and inside her chest, her heart boomed like a bass drum.

Even Scotti couldn't help her now. They had planned for Scotti to come over alone, but her mother had been waiting at the curb and reminded Scotti that she had an appointment at the dentist after school.

Lorna's faint hope that someone in the Markham family might have come home early was extinguished the instant they entered the quiet house.

Just in case, she called out, "Mom! Tiffy! Skip! Anybody home?"

No one answered.

"Looks as if we've got the place to ourselves," said Mike.

She was sorry she had called out. Now he knew for certain that they were alone.

He reached out and took her hand. "I know which subject we should study first."

Lorna pulled her hand away from his and hurried toward the kitchen. "Let's get something to eat. I don't know about you, but I'm starved."

Mike followed her into the kitchen. "I hope you aren't planning to make pizza again. Let's have something that's quick so we can get back to business."

She swallowed hard. "Yeah, I've got *tons* of homework."

Lorna glanced up at the clock over the kitchen table: 4:05. It was almost an hour before anyone else would be home. Making a mad dash to the refrigerator, she began pulling out cans of soda, cold cuts, cheese, pickles, mustard, and ketchup. She loaded them onto the counter and went back for bread.

"Do you like lettuce on your sandwich?" she asked.

Mike shook his head. "Takes too much time. Besides, I'm not really hungry. I'll just have something to drink."

He picked up a soda can and popped the top. She could feel him watching her over the rim of the can while he took a sip. Then he set the can on the counter and came up behind her. He put his arms around her and softly kissed her cheek, sending an unbelievable thrill racing through her.

"You don't really want a sandwich, do you?" he asked in a dreamy voice. "We've got more important things to do."

As the thrill subsided, she looked at the pile of sandwich makings on the counter and shook her head. She knew the sandwich routine wasn't going to work.

She moved away from him, grabbed the other can of soda, and headed back to the family room, plastering a bright smile on her face. "How about some music. I love to study to music. My brother Skip has an awesome collection of CDs. Why don't you look through them and pick out something."

Mike glanced at the stack of CDs and back to her. "Lorna, why are you stalling?"

The question jolted her. "Stalling? What do you mean, 'stalling'?"

"You know exactly what I mean," said Mike. "If you don't like me, just say so and I'll leave. But I thought you did like me. I thought we really had something going."

"Of course I like you, Mike," Lorna insisted. He was looking at her with such a sad expression that it almost broke her heart. "I like you a lot. It's just that . . ."

"It's just that *what*?" he pressed, pulling her close to him again. He tipped her chin upward and bent close to kiss her.

She felt herself swaying toward him. With all her heart she wanted to kiss him, but an instant before his lips could brush hers, she pushed him away.

"I just can't do this. Not yet," she said. "You're coming on too fast, Mike. I'm just not ready. You've got to understand."

Mike's eyes flashed with anger and disbelief. "Yeah. Sure," he muttered.

Lorna wanted desperately to say something to make everything all right again, but she didn't know what to say. Silently she watched him grab his books and storm out of the house, slamming the door.

.  .  .

# THE GREAT DAD DISASTER

The phone was ringing when Scotti and her mother got home from the dentist. It was Lorna, and she was crying as she told Scotti about her fight with Mike.

"I know he'll never ask me out again," Lorna said through her tears. "I've lost him."

"Boys," grumbled Scotti. "If you ask me, Mike would respect your feelings if he likes you as much as he says he does."

Lorna sighed. "I know, Scotti. I think about that sometimes, too. But I like him so much. I've never met anybody like him before."

"Sure, but is he worth losing your self-respect?" asked Scotti.

"I know what you're saying, but . . . but I can't take the chance."

After they hung up, Scotti thought about Lorna's situation. She's always so down on herself. If she had more self-confidence, she'd be able to stand up to Mike without worrying that she'd lose him, thought Scotti.

She drummed her fingers on the telephone. She was tempted to call Lorna back and tell her Mike wasn't worth it. Not if he couldn't accept her limits.

No, she decided. That would only make her mad at me. She's going to have to make her own decision.

. . .

Every day Lorna told Scotti that Mike had ignored her. He avoided her in the halls. And the only telephone calls she got at home were from Scotti.

What a jerk, Scotti thought. It was depressing to see Lorna so sad. The only thing that made Scotti feel happy was looking forward to her Friday night date with Cary.

Then her dad struck again.

He had gotten home on Wednesday, and she had waited until Thursday at the dinner table to tell him she had a date with Cary on Friday night.

"I knew it would be okay to tell him I could go," Scotti said confidently. "We haven't been together since last weekend, and you said we could go out once a week."

"I did some checking around, and he seems to be from a good family," her father said. "His dad has an insurance agency, and his mother works at a day-care center."

"What!" shrieked Scotti. "You checked around? Do you mean you spied on them? Dad, how could you?"

"It's my duty as your father," he replied indignantly. "And I didn't spy on them. I just talked to some friends who live in the Calheims' neighborhood. There are a lot of crazies out there, Scotti. You can't be too careful."

"Now you're saying you thought Cary's parents might be crazies!" she shouted, jumping to her feet. "If Cary ever finds out you did that, I'll die. It will be the most humiliating moment of my life!"

"Calm down, Scotti. I didn't say you couldn't go out with him. Will Mr. Markham be driving you again?"

His question stopped Scotti cold. She took a deep breath and shook her head. "Lorna and Mike aren't going out," she said. "They broke up."

"Mmmm," he said, nodding. "Lorna's a sensible girl. She probably decided that she's not ready to date."

"That's not exactly the problem," Scotti said, avoiding her father's eyes.

"Well, whatever the reason, it's probably for the best," her father said. "And if Coy Markham isn't going to drive, I will. Just let me know what time you two would like to leave for the theater."

Scotti looked at her father in horror.

Oh, no! she thought. Please don't let this be happening!

# 16

After Scotti thought about it, the idea that her dad was driving them to the movie didn't seem so bad after all. It might be a great opportunity for her father to see how nice Cary really was.

"Why don't you tell him some of the great things about yourself that you told me," Scotti suggested to Cary when they were talking together after school on Friday.

He gave her a blank look. "Like what?"

"I think Dad would be impressed with the story of why you decided to become a veterinarian. You know, about how you tried to save your little dog Goofy and couldn't. Dad's awfully softhearted when it comes to animals."

Cary looked doubtful, so she went on quickly before he could argue.

"And another thing, you could mention how long and hard you've been working on your car and that you're paying for it yourself with money you've earned. He'd get the picture that you're mature and responsible. Hey, listen. If you could throw in something about how close you and your dad have gotten from working together, it would knock his socks off!"

"Scotti! I can't talk about that. It would sound like I'm bragging," Cary insisted.

"You told me, and I didn't think you were bragging," said Scotti.

"Yeah, but that was different," said Cary.

"Okay, if you're too chicken to try to impress him, I'll have to think of a way to do it," Scotti said confidently.

By the time Cary arrived at six-thirty, she had buttered up her dad so much that he was in a fabulous mood, but Cary looked as nervous as ever.

"Relax, everything's cool," she whispered when she answered the door. "Dad's in a great mood tonight."

Cary gave her a skeptical look and came inside. She saw him take a deep breath before he spoke. "Hello, Mr. Wheeler."

"Hi, Cary," her father said pleasantly.

The strain of being around her father showed on Cary's face.

"You kids go on to the car. I just have to get my keys."

Mr. Wheeler disappeared down the hall, and

Cary followed Scotti out to the car, which was parked at the curb.

"As soon as he comes out, rush over and open the back car door for me to get in," Scotti instructed. "If I know Dad, he'll be impressed with your politeness."

A moment later Mr. Wheeler came out of the house. He wasn't exactly smiling, but he wasn't frowning either. Scotti crossed her fingers and prayed that her plan would work.

Cary went into action. He reached out for the door handle, but it was obviously farther away than he had thought. He leaned past Scotti and suddenly tripped on the curb, bumping against her and pinning her to the side of the car with all of his weight.

Everything happened in a flash for Scotti. At the same instant that Cary seemed to grab her in a giant hug, her father's mouth dropped open and his face clouded up in a frown.

"What's going on?" he shouted. "Cary Calheim! Get away from my daughter!"

Cary's face was purple as they untangled themselves.

"It's okay, Dad," said Scotti. "Cary was just trying to open the car door for me, and he tripped."

"That's right, sir," Cary mumbled. "I'm sorry if it looked . . ."

# THE GREAT DAD DISASTER

From the expression on his face, Scotti knew that he was too mortified to finish the sentence.

Her father wasn't helping matters. He was glaring at Cary, and she could almost read what he was thinking.

"Come on. Let's get into the car," she said, trying to sound as if nothing had happened.

Cary followed her into the backseat, and her father got behind the wheel. It was a long, silent ride to the movie theater.

"There's no need to call me when you're ready to come home. I'll pick you up in front of Rudy's at ten-thirty *sharp!*" her father called when they got out of the car.

As soon as they got into the theater, Scotti relaxed. Cary loosened up, too. They got popcorn, found seats, and then sat back to enjoy the movie.

"Since your father's driving tonight, it's a good thing Rex didn't offer us his car," said Cary as they followed the crowd heading for Rudy's after the show.

"Ooh, you're right," said Scotti. She shivered at the thought of her dad catching her cruising around with Cary and Rex. "I'm surprised he isn't here already."

"Don't even think that," said Cary. "Now I'll be watching for him the rest of the night."

They drifted into Rudy's with the crowd and found a small table that was vacant. Scotti busied herself greeting her friends.

"Hi, Brianna. Hi, Jami. Hi, Missy," she called out and waved in several directions.

They ordered Cokes and talked to a few kids who stopped by their table.

"Want to play some video games?" asked Cary.

Scotti looked at her watch. "Better not. It's only ten minutes until Dad's supposed to be here."

"Before he gets here, there's some-thing . . ." Cary began and paused. He looked away from her, as if he couldn't make himself finish the sentence.

"What is it, Cary?" Scotti asked. "Is some-thing wrong?"

He flashed a big smile. "No, nothing's wrong. Honest."

She watched his dimple fade away with his smile, and wondered what he had started to say and if it was about her father.

"I'm really sorry my dad was so unreal again," she said. "It's hard to figure him out. He's pretty cool most of the time, but—"

"Scotti! Come here a minute. We need to talk to you."

**110**

Scotti looked around to see Brianna waving at her. "Come on," she called again. "It's important."

Scotti glanced at her watch. It was only five minutes now until her father would drive up outside. But Brianna had said it was important.

"I'll be back in a minute," she said to Cary.

"Is it true that Lorna and Mike broke up?" Brianna asked the instant Scotti slid into the booth beside her.

"Well . . . I guess so," said Scotti. "He didn't ask her out for this weekend."

"See, I told you," Missy said to Brianna. Turning back to Scotti, she said, "That's not all. I saw him flirting with Holly Hooper in the cafeteria today."

Scotti shrugged. She didn't like to hear people gossiping about Lorna, and she wanted to change the subject. "I really don't know anything about it," she said.

"Right," Missy said sarcastically. "She's only your best friend."

Suddenly there was a commotion near the front door. Scotti spun around to see what was going on.

"Oh, my gosh. It's Cary, and he's yelling at the waitress," said Brianna. "Scotti, you'd better find out what's going on."

Scotti was already on her way to the front of the restaurant. The waitress was holding a glass of Coke out of Cary's reach. It looked like Scotti's glass of Coke.

"Cary! What's happening?" she cried.

Around the room, kids stopped their conversations to see what was going on. Before Cary could answer, the front door opened and a policeman strode in.

"Cary!" she cried again, running to his side. "Are you okay?"

Just then the door opened again and her father rushed in. Scotti gasped.

"What's going on?" demanded Mr. Wheeler. "There's a police car with flashing lights outside, and my daughter's in here!"

Ignoring Scotti's father, the waitress handed the glass to the policeman. "Thanks for responding so quickly, Officer. This glass of Coke belonged to *her*," she said, pointing to Scotti. "And when her back was turned, I saw *him* drop something into it. I think it was drugs."

Scotti felt her knees go weak. The room was deathly silent as all eyes turned to Cary.

# 17

Lorna was in a deep sleep when the phone rang. She rubbed her eyes and looked at the clock on her bedside table: 11:32. Maybe it was her parents, calling to tell her they would be out later than they had expected.

"Hello?"

"Oh, Lorna! I'm so glad you're up! Wait until I tell you what happened!" Scotti said breathlessly.

"Whoa, slow down," said Lorna. "Is everything okay?"

"It is now," said Scotti, "but talk about a *disaster*!"

Lorna listened in amazement as Scotti told her the story. "Drugs!" Lorna cried. "Oh, my gosh, Scotti!"

"Yeah, I thought my dad would go into cardiac arrest when the waitress said that," she said.

"Then the policeman calmly asked the waitress to get him a clean glass. He poured the Coke very slowly from my glass into the clean glass, and you'll never believe what was in the bottom."

"You mean Cary really had put something in your Coke?" Lorna asked incredulously.

"Yes! I can't wait for you to see it. It's this really beautiful gold pinkie ring with interlocking hearts! He said he'd been trying all evening to get up his nerve to give it to me. By then it was time for my dad to pick us up, and he knew he couldn't give it to me in front of him. So when I left the table for a minute, he dropped it into my Coke, thinking that when I came back I'd find it."

"Cool! But did he have to explain all that in front of your dad?" asked Lorna.

"Yeah, in front of my dad, the policeman, the waitress, and all the kids in Rudy's. I think he's got terminal embarrassment," said Scotti. "And the thing that makes it all so crazy is that Cary is really a cool guy, but he has this talent for coming off wrong in front of my dad. You notice this didn't happen the night *your* dad drove."

"So what did your dad say?"

Scotti chuckled. "It's weird, but he didn't say a thing. I think he was just relieved that it was a ring instead of drugs."

Lorna stared sadly into space. Jealousy was

**114**

settling on her like a dark fog. She tried to push it away, but she couldn't.

"I guess that means Cary really likes you," she said. "I wish Mike still liked me."

Scotti bit her tongue. It was the perfect time to tell Lorna how she felt about Mike. But Lorna might not take it the way she meant it. Instead she said, "He may be mad at you now, but it won't take him long to realize what a great girlfriend he has."

Lorna sighed. "I hope you're right."

After they hung up, Lorna sank back on her pillow and stared at the ceiling, thinking about Mike. She had gone over and over their big fight, and there was one thing she couldn't understand. He had accused her of not liking him. How could he say a thing like that? She liked him more than any boy she had ever known. Didn't he know that there was more to liking a boy than kissing him?

And even if Mike did come back, things would probably be the same, she thought. He would pressure her again. And he would have plenty of chances since her father gave them so much freedom.

Scotti doesn't realize how lucky she is, Lorna thought. If Cary came on too strong, all she would have to do is say, my dad says I've got to go home now. He would believe her.

The girls had made plans to go to the football game together the next afternoon, and Scotti was all giggly and bubbly as she showed Lorna her ring when Lorna arrived at her house after lunch.

"Isn't it gorgeous?" she said, sticking out her pinkie finger and twisting her hand from side to side as she admired it. "I mean, look at how the twin hearts are carved so that they're locked together. It's sooo romantic! I guess I finally beat out my biggest competition—his car."

Lorna looked away so that Scotti wouldn't see the jealousy in her eyes. Just a week ago she'd been on cloud nine herself, and she knew how special the feeling was.

"We'd better get going," she murmured.

As soon as the door to Scotti's house closed behind them, Scotti stopped and put a hand on Lorna's arm.

"Lorna, I need to ask you a big favor, and I couldn't do it in front of my dad," she said just above a whisper. "Cary wants to take me to the game, but Dad hasn't given in on his one-date-per-week rule. I told Cary I'd leave the house with you and meet him at the corner of Seventh and Foxfire and then go on to the game with him. That way Dad won't know I'm not with you. I know it's sneaking around, and I hate to ask you, but you don't really mind, do you?" Scotti asked with pleading eyes. "I'd do the same for you."

Lorna couldn't believe what she was hearing. Scotti was using her. Dumping her for a stupid boy after all they had been through together.

"Go ahead! Sneak around," she snapped. "I don't care what you do. You can *elope* for all I care!"

She stomped down the sidewalk without looking back. It was a chilly fall afternoon, and there was an icy bite to the wind as she headed for the stadium. Tears stung her eyes, and her heart felt as if it would burst.

Scotti watched Lorna storm away. She knew she should go after her and apologize, but she couldn't. The most terrible thing was that she didn't know *why* she couldn't. Lorna was her best friend. And she knew Lorna was hurt. But her legs wouldn't move. They were rooted to the spot.

Besides, I *have* to go to the game with Cary today, she rationalized. He just gave me the ring last night. And everyone will be talking about what happened at Rudy's.

Scotti waited until Lorna was out of sight, and then she hurried to meet Cary.

# 18

Lorna zipped up her jacket. The cold wind was making her shiver.

Maybe I should just go back home, she thought, walking slowly toward the stadium. Who wants to freeze to death to watch some stupid football game? Besides, who am I going to sit with? Scotti will be with Cary. Brianna, Missy, and Jami will probably be there, but maybe they won't, and I'll have to sit by myself. I should definitely go back home!

Then she thought about Mike. Seeing his face in her mind made her heart ache. Being his girlfriend had been so much fun while it lasted. If only it could happen again.

There was a long line at the ticket booth, but she didn't see any of her friends.

I could still duck out, she thought. No one would care anyway. Especially Mike.

# THE GREAT DAD DISASTER

As she got closer to the ticket booth, Lorna glanced at the line forming behind her. Still no sign of Brianna or Missy or Jami.

Why don't I just leave? she wondered as she paid for her ticket.

Inside the gate she spotted Brianna at the refreshment stand and hurried to her.

"Hi, Lorna," said Brianna. "I don't know about you, but I'm freezing. It's going to be miserable in the stands."

"Yeah, I almost chickened out and went back home," said Lorna. "Can I sit with you guys? We can huddle together to keep warm."

Brianna chuckled. "Sure. Where's Scotti? Did you guys come together?"

Lorna shook her head. "She's with Cary."

The girls bought cups of hot chocolate and headed toward the stands where Missy and Jami were holding seats.

"It's too bad about you and Mike," said Missy as soon as Lorna sat down. "Have you seen him hanging around with Holly Hooper as much as I have this week? She's the world's biggest flirt."

Lorna didn't answer. She hoped her face didn't give away how miserable she felt. It was bad enough to lose him, but to Holly Hooper of all people!

"Hanging *all over her* is more like it, if you ask me," said Jami. "Honestly, Lorna, you'd better do something and do it fast if you want to get him back."

"I totally agree," said Brianna.

"But what?" Lorna asked desperately.

"That's *easy*," said Brianna. "Figure out what made him mad in the first place and do the opposite."

Lorna felt her face flush with embarrassment. She was glad that no one was looking at her. The band had started playing the school fight song and everyone was standing up to cheer as the cheerleaders led the team onto the field.

Brianna doesn't know what she's suggesting, Lorna thought. I could never do a thing like that.

She got slowly to her feet and looked down on the field. The sight of Mike made her heart break. He looked more handsome than ever in his white pants and red and white letter sweater. The crowd applauded wildly when he finished his tumbling run.

Then Holly ran up to Mike. He grabbed her and tossed her over his head. She spun in the air and made a perfect landing on his shoulders. He swayed slightly to steady himself, and they held out their arms to the crowd.

Tears blurred Lorna's eyes as she watched

their perfectly synchronized performance and thought how great they looked together. Then Mike dropped Holly lightly to the ground, and they held hands as the crowd cheered again.

Brianna nudged Lorna in the ribs. "Look at that witch!"

Lorna didn't want to look, but she couldn't help it. Holly stretched up on tiptoes and planted a big kiss on Mike's cheek.

"You aren't going to let her get away with that, are you?" demanded Jami.

Lorna took a deep breath and let it out slowly, glaring down at Holly as she flirted outrageously with Mike. Maybe Brianna had the right idea after all. Maybe she shouldn't resist Mike so completely. Maybe she had been a *prude*.

"You've got it right," she replied with determination. "I'm going to get him back if it's the last thing I ever do."

It turned out to be a miserable afternoon. The temperature dropped steadily, and Colleyville lost twenty-four to nothing.

A chilly rain had begun to fall when Lorna said good-bye to her friends and headed toward the exit. Her mood was gloomier than the weather. Holly had flirted with Mike all through the game, and he had seemed to enjoy it. Lorna's resolve to get him back had evaporated into thin air. There was no use trying. He belonged to Holly Hooper now.

She was almost to the exit when she felt someone looking at her. Stopping, she glanced around. To her amazement, she locked eyes with Mike. He was just inside the gate staring straight at her. He was also with Holly. She was checking her hair in a small hand mirror.

Mike wasn't smiling, but he was looking at her so intently that she couldn't look away.

He wants me to say something, she thought. Panic grabbed her. Here's my chance. If I'm going to get him back, I've got to do it *now*.

By this time Holly had noticed Lorna and was frowning furiously at her.

Lorna tried her best to ignore Holly. Her stomach was churning. "Hi, Mike," she called out.

A slow smile spread across his face. "Hi, Lorna. How's it going?"

She relaxed a little. "Great."

*Now what can I say!* a voice screamed in her head. Her eyes flicked toward Holly for an instant and then back to Mike. "Can I talk to you a minute in private?"

"Sure," said Mike, heading toward her.

Behind him, Lorna could see Holly angrily put her hands on her hips and glare at them.

"I was just wondering if you'd like to come

over after school Monday . . . and study," she asked. It took every bit of willpower she had to keep her voice from shaking.

Mike didn't say anything for a moment, and Lorna felt another stab of panic.

"Well . . . sure," he said slowly. "If you really want me to."

"I do," she said before she could lose her nerve. "See you then."

I did it! she thought triumphantly. But as she raced toward home, dread over what would happen Monday loomed over her like a dark storm cloud.

Scotti was bursting with happiness when she got home from the game.

I need to tell someone how much fun I had and what a super person Cary is. *Beyond* super! she thought. But who can I tell?

Her spirits tumbled as she thought about Lorna. She hated it that their friendship was falling apart. It was awful to not have anyone to talk to.

She went to her closet and pulled the key to her diary out of its hiding place. At least she could still talk to her diary.

When she opened it, she was amazed at how long it had been since she had written in it.

I guess I've just been too busy, she thought.

*123*

*Dear Diary,*
      *Cary gets more wonderful every time I'm with him. Last night he gave me a pinkie ring with interlocking hearts carved on it, and today*

Scotti put down her pen and gazed out her window. Beyond the stockade fence stood the Markhams' two-story house. She could see Lorna's bedroom window in the upper-left corner.

She closed her diary with a sigh. "It's just not the same as talking to Lorna," she whispered and reached for the phone.

# 19

Scotti paced the floor, waiting for Lorna. She was unbelievably nervous about facing her best friend. She didn't have the slightest idea what she was going to say.

When a soft tap sounded at her bedroom door, she jumped a foot.

"Come in," she called.

Lorna entered the room. The hurt look that Scotti had seen on her face in the driveway was still there. Lorna stood just inside the door, but she didn't say anything or take off her jacket.

Scotti's pulse was racing. She was losing her best friend, and she needed to say exactly the right thing.

"I'm sorry about today," she blurted out. "I know what I did was wrong, but I just couldn't help it. I knew I should run after you and tell you I was sorry, but my legs wouldn't move. Being with Cary was so *important*. And then I started thinking that if you're really my best friend, you'd understand. You'd want me to be with Cary."

"Don't you know that I felt used!" Lorna snapped. "As if the only thing I'm good for is to trick your dad so you can be with Cary. But what about me? You just dumped me. You didn't wonder if I would have anybody to sit with at the game or anything. All you thought about was *yourself*. And your *boyfriend*!"

Lorna's words stung. Scotti started to lash back at her, but she caught herself and looked solemnly at Lorna.

"I think you've just hit the problem on the head," Scotti said quietly. "Boyfriends. They change everything. They take over. I haven't been able to think about anything but Cary since I first laid eyes on him. I've quit talking to my parents, except when it's absolutely necessary. My homework is slipping. It's crazy! And nothing has been the same between us since we met Cary and Mike."

"You can say that again," mumbled Lorna. "Since you've been going with Cary, you never have time for me. We used to be together all the time, and when we weren't together, we talked on the phone. But all that's changed now. The only time you call me is to brag about something Cary's done. All you *ever* talk about is Cary. I might as well not exist."

"What about how things were while you and Mike were going out?" retorted Scotti. "How often did you call me?"

Lorna hesitated and tears welled up in her eyes. "I . . . you're right. I guess I got carried away, too. But I really miss having you to talk to. You know, about important things. I need your advice right now, but you're never around."

A lump filled Scotti's throat. She really did miss being close to Lorna. Cary was great, but there were some things you simply couldn't talk over with a boy. You needed a best girlfriend.

"You can talk to me," she said softly. "I promise I'll *always* be your best friend. And I'll never forget it again, even if Cary and I fall madly in love and get married someday. You'll be able to talk to me forever."

Lorna gave her a teary smile. "I'll be your best friend forever, too. And if I seem to be ignoring you or your problems because of Mike, remind me. Okay?"

"Okay," promised Scotti, "and you do the same for me."

Later, when they had talked and even giggled for a while, Scotti turned serious again.

127

"You said you need some advice. Is it something you want to talk about now?"

Lorna nodded. "The sooner the better. It's about Mike. You know how much I like him, and you know why he stopped asking me out. I know what I did was right, but . . ."

"But what?" asked Scotti.

"But what if I was overreacting and Mike had a right to get mad? I mean, all he did was try to kiss me. That's *all*! I swear he didn't try anything else. I was just being a total prude, and that's why I lost him." Lorna looked at Scotti defiantly.

"So, am I getting this straight? Now you think that what you did was wrong instead of right?" asked Scotti.

Lorna looked as if she were about to burst into tears. "Oh, Scotti, I don't know if what I did was right or wrong. I'm *so* confused. I can see it both ways. And I like Mike so much and want him back. And that witch Holly Hooper is out to get him."

"Yeah, that's pretty obvious," said Scotti. "I couldn't help noticing them at the game."

"Now you see what I'm up against," said Lorna. "I'm sure he really liked me, but I'm sure he could get anything he wants from Holly and probably a dozen other girls. That's why . . ."

# THE GREAT DAD DISASTER

She hesitated and looked at Scotti with uncertainty. "That's why I invited him over to do homework Monday after school."

"What!" shrieked Scotti. Her eyes popped open wide, and she stared at Lorna in disbelief. "You mean you're going to let him . . ." She couldn't finish the question.

"That's the problem," Lorna insisted. She looked at Scotti with pleading eyes. "I don't know what I'm going to do. I don't want to go too far, but I want him back so badly." She lowered her voice to just above a whisper. "If he comes over and I lose him again, I know this time it will be forever. That's why I need your advice."

Scotti was reeling with shock. This is a major problem, she thought. *Beyond* major. How can I possibly know the right thing to say?

# 20

Lorna couldn't help feeling a little disappointed in Scotti's advice. Still, she thought, what else could she say?

"I don't think you'd like yourself very much if you went very far," Scotti had said. "But you're the only one who really knows what's right for you."

Lorna tossed and turned all Saturday night trying to figure out what really was right for her. By morning, instead of a solution to her problem, she had a stuffy nose and a raw, scratchy throat. As the day progressed, so did her cold.

"Sweetheart, you look flushed. I think you have a fever," Mrs. Markham said at lunch. She reached across the table and touched Lorna's cheeks and forehead. "I was right. As soon as you're finished eating I'll load you up with cold medicine and tuck you into bed."

## THE GREAT DAD DISASTER

A little while later Lorna crawled into bed and pulled the covers up, happy to be there. She felt awful. And terribly tired. She snuggled deep into the bed and was almost asleep when the phone rang. She ignored it, but a moment later Tiffany burst into her room.

"Are you awake, Lorna? It's Scotti, and she wants to talk to you."

"I'b awake now," Lorna mumbled. Propping herself up on an elbow, she picked up the receiver on her bedside table. "Hi, Scotti. What's ub?"

"Is that you, Lorna? You sound funny," said Scotti.

"I'b got a code," she replied. "A bad code. I ache all ober. I can't breathe. I'b sneezed until my stomach's sore. I'b a bess."

"Are you chickening out, or are you really sick?" Scotti asked in a skeptical voice.

"What do you mean, ab I chickening out?" Lorna asked indignantly.

"It's pretty obvious to me that if you're too sick to go to school tomorrow, you'll be too sick for Mike to come over. That way you can put off having to deal with him a little longer, and he can't possibly get mad."

"Why didn't I think of that?" Lorna cried. "Thanks a billion."

"You're more than welcome," said Scotti. "Now maybe you can return the favor and come up with an idea for me."

"What's wrog?"

"It's Dad again!" Scotti said, heaving a big sigh. "I just couldn't believe how quiet he and Mom have been about the ring Cary gave me. Dad was there when Cary fished it out of the glass and handed it to me, and I showed it to Mom as soon as she got home Sunday. She just said that it was very pretty. Period. No comment from either of them. Until today."

"Uh-oh. What habbened?" Lorna asked.

"Dad was awfully quiet at breakfast. Like he had something on his mind. A little while later he came to my room and launched into this big speech about how other kids would see the ring Cary gave me and think that we were going steady and how we were definitely too young for that."

She paused. "That was bad enough, right? Next he said that since he and Mom were allowing me to date now, I should date other boys besides Cary, and—get this—if I want to go on a date this coming weekend, it has to be with a different boy. *Can you believe that?*"

"Scotti! That's awful! What did you say?"

"I argued with him. I asked him if he expected *me* to ask some other boy out. When he wouldn't give in, I said something snotty about how if I did what he said, he'd have to spend all his spare time spying on the other boys' families the way he did on Cary's. I shouldn't have said that. He blew his cool and threatened to ground me until the year 2000 for having a smart mouth, but so far he hasn't. What am I going to do, Lorna? I don't want to go out with anybody except Cary."

"Well, for starters, you'd better get on your dad's good side again," said Lorna. "I can't believe you said that about spying."

"I know," Scotti said dejectedly. "Sometimes I just open my mouth and seriously weird things come out. Anyway, I'd really appreciate it if you could help me think of a way to talk Dad out of this dating-other-boys garbage—and before this weekend. Okay?" she asked urgently.

"Sure," said Lorna. "I'll try by best. Gotta go now. I think I'b going to sneeze."

For the rest of the day, Lorna ate chicken soup and took all the decongestants, cough syrup, and aspirin her mother brought to her. She hardly noticed how much her mother fussed over her because her mind was constantly on Mike.

He's so handsome, and so sweet, and I really

do like kissing him. But if he comes over tomorrow after school, how far will he expect me to go? she wondered. Maybe I made a mistake inviting him over. What if he gets the wrong idea? And if I make him mad again I'll lose him forever! He'll go straight to Holly Hooper!

Lorna pounded her pillow in frustration. Surely I'll still be too sick to go to school tomorrow, she thought. And I'll be able to stall him a little longer.

When Lorna awoke the next morning, she was horrified at how good she felt. No more stuffy nose. No more scratchy throat. The achy feeling was gone. She was well!

"Oh, no!" she cried. She jumped out of bed in a panic and raced to her dresser mirror. Her eyes were no longer pink and puffy, but there was still a little redness around her nose from blowing it so often.

Can I fake it? she wondered desperately.

She was still at the mirror, practicing various ways of looking miserable, when she heard her mother coming up the steps. She dived for the bed and yanked up the covers just as her mother opened the door.

"So how are you feeling this mornin', sweetheart?" Mrs. Markham asked cheerfully. "My, you do look a lot better. Must have been a twenty-four-hour bug. It's a good thing I gave you all that medicine and my homemade chicken soup. Does the trick every time."

"I really don't feel that good yet," Lorna said in the weakest voice she could. Then thinking fast, she added, "I've got a bad headache, and I woke up in the night with chills. I don't think I'd better go to school today, Mom."

Her heart was pounding as her mother sat down on the side of the bed and looked at her closely. Mrs. Markham smoothed the long dark hair away from her face and felt her cheeks and forehead.

Her mother frowned and stood up. "You don't feel hot. You're breathing normally. I think you'll feel better when you're up and moving around. Come on, sweetheart, rise and shine. It's a school day."

"But Mo-*oom,*" she agonized. "I really don't feel well enough to go to school. And besides, you don't want the whole school to catch what I've got, do you?"

"I don't understand why you're trying to get out of school this morning," said Mrs. Markham, shaking her head. "If you're having some sort of problem with a teacher or a classmate that's making you want to stay home, let's talk about it."

"No problem," Lorna murmured.

She sank against the pillow and watched her mother leave the room. Why did I take all that medicine? she wondered miserably. Why didn't I hide those pills under my pillow so that I wouldn't get well so fast? But I didn't. I took them, and now I don't have any choice. I have to go to school and face Mike.

# 21

"**W**hat are you doing here?" asked Scotti at the bus stop. "I thought you were too sick to go to school today."

"Don't I wish," said Lorna. "I did something stupid. I took all the medicine Mom gave me yesterday, and I'm *well*!"

"Oh, no," said Scotti. "So what about Mike?"

"Do you think I haven't been worrying about that? I'm so nervous I can't think straight. You don't have any more brilliant ideas, do you?" Lorna said dejectedly as they climbed onto the bus.

Scotti shook her head. "Not unless you can figure out a way to have a relapse. You sounded awful on the phone yesterday. I wouldn't have come near you for anything."

Lorna stared out the bus window. I could always tell him that I don't want him to come home with me after school, she thought sadly. And then when he asked me why, I could tell him the truth, that he wants to make out too much.

She sighed, knowing what Mike would do next. He would get mad all over again and go running straight to Holly Hooper. It was a no-win situation any way she looked at it.

By the end of the school day, she was a nervous wreck. She had seen Mike twice in the halls, and he had given her a big grin each time. In math class he passed her a note that said, *See you after school!*

Now her knees were shaking as she waited for him by the front door. It was time to face the music.

"If only I hadn't gotten well so fast," she muttered. "If only there was a pill I could take to make me sick again."

Suddenly Scotti's words came back to her.

*"Not unless you can figure out a way to have a relapse. You sounded awful on the phone yesterday. I wouldn't have come near you for anything."*

That's it! she thought. Scotti doesn't know it, but she came through for me again. I'll have a relapse. I can't have a real one, so I'll fake it!

Ducking into the girls' bathroom, she did a

quick survey of herself in the mirror. Rats, she thought. I look even less sick than I did this morning.

Pulling out her lipstick, she dabbed a little of the soft pink color on each cheek to make herself look flushed and feverish. The raw redness around her nose had faded, too, so she added a tiny bit of color. She mussed her hair slightly and practiced again the expressions of misery. They hadn't worked on her mother this morning, but there was still a chance they might work on Mike.

She grabbed a couple of paper towels and stuffed them into her jacket pocket. "I think I'm ready now," she whispered. Taking a deep breath, she opened the door.

Mike was waiting for her on the front steps. He flashed a big smile when she came out, reaching for her hand.

"Hi, Bike," she called out cheerfully, slipping her hand inside his. Sounding as if she had a stuffy nose was easy to fake.

Mike gave her a surprised look as they started down the street. "Am I hearing things, or did you call me Bike?"

"Oh, sorry about that," she said. "I hab a code. I spent most of the day yesterday in bed."

"Oh," he said.

She pulled a paper towel out of her jacket

pocket and blew her nose loudly. "I'b really a lot better today," she assured him. "I was sneezing my head off yesterday. I was a total bess."

"Yeah, well . . . I'm glad you're feeling better."

Lorna could hear uncertainty in his voice. It's working! she thought and coughed a couple of times for effect.

"And I'b glad that you're cobing over today," she said.

Mike stopped walking and turned toward her. "Yeah, well," he began slowly. "I probably should let you go on home by yourself and get some more rest. I know you don't feel very good, and I'd hate to make you worse. It's okay, isn't it? You won't get mad, will you?"

Lorna gave him one of her miserable looks and said, "Ob course not, if that's what *you* really want to do."

Relief spread across Mike's face. "It's not what I want to do. It's what I think's best. See you tomorrow. Okay?" Hesitating, he added, "And, Lorna . . . if you think you'll be well by Friday night, I'd like to take you out."

"That would be great," she answered.

"Bye," he said, turning to leave again.

"Bye, Mike," she said and caught herself.

She held her breath, but if he heard her call him Mike instead of Bike, he didn't let it show.

I haven't lost him yet! she thought joyfully. There's still time for a miracle!

Scotti had kept an eye on the clock ever since she got off the bus. Had Lorna and Mike gotten to her house yet? she wondered. If they had, how was Lorna handling the situation?

It was all she could do to keep from calling and asking Lorna questions that could be answered yes or no or sneaking across their adjoining backyards and peeking in the windows. Or maybe she should go over to Lorna's house and barge in. She knew she could never do any of those things, of course, but the suspense was killing her just the same.

When the phone rang, she grabbed the receiver. "Hello!"

"Hi, Scotti, it's me!"

"Wow, Lorna, you sound happy. Did everything go okay?"

"Did it ever, and it was all because of you." She explained how she'd remembered what Scotti had said about a relapse and had faked being sick.

"I think he was afraid I'd breathe on him and he'd catch something fatal," Lorna said and giggled. "You should have seen how far he backed away when I called him Bike instead of Mike and then started blowing my nose. But the best part is, he still likes me. He asked me out for Friday night."

"Lucky you," Scotti said sadly. Then she quickly added, "I'm really glad. I'm sorry if I sounded a little jealous. I guess I am. Dad still says I have to go out with a different boy this weekend or else not go out at all, and I don't know what to do."

"I know what you can do," Lorna said confidently. "This time *I'm* the one with the brilliant idea. We'll double again, and you can tell your dad you're going out with Mike. He can come to the door to get you and everything."

Scotti was too stunned to speak for a moment. "It's perfect," she said excitedly. "But do you think Mike will go along with it?"

"Why not?" asked Lorna. "When we explain the situation to Mike and Cary, they'll think it's a blast. And listen, why don't you plan to spend the night at my house? That way Mike won't have to face the 'D.D.' when we get home."

"The 'D.D.'?" asked Scotti. "What's that?"

"The Dreaded Dad," responded Lorna in a sinister voice.

They both went into a fit of laughter.

Lorna is the best friend anybody could ever have! Scotti thought when they hung up.

It was a perfect plan. She was going to be with Cary. And her dad would never find out.

# 22

"**W**hat did I tell you? Getting a date with another boy wasn't so hard, was it?" Mr. Wheeler asked when Scotti announced that she would be going to the movie on Friday night with a boy named Mike Kilpatrick.

Scotti almost couldn't stand it that her father thought he had won a big victory. But she was relieved that he didn't seem to recognize Mike's name.

Now, as she waited for Mike, she realized he would have to face both her parents tonight because her mother had gotten home earlier in the day and her father didn't leave on his next flight until tomorrow.

When the doorbell rang, she threw a nervous glance toward the family room where her parents were waiting and yanked the door open.

"Hi, Mike," she said. He looked frightened. Whispering, she added, "We're going to make this fast. Just a quick hello and good-bye and we're outta here!"

Mike pulled himself up straight and said, "Okay. Let's get it over with."

Scotti led him into the family room where her parents were reading the evening paper.

"Mom, Dad, this is Mike Kilpatrick," she said.

Her mother looked up and smiled. Her dad took off his reading glasses and slowly looked Mike up and down.

"Hello, Mike," said Mrs. Wheeler. "We're very happy to meet you."

"Um . . . same here, ma'am," Mike sputtered.

Her father frowned. "Mike Kilpatrick. Ever since Scotti mentioned that she was going out with you I've been trying to remember where I've heard your name before. Do you play sports?"

Scotti threw him a warning look.

"No, sir."

"Come on, Mike. We'd better hurry," Scotti said. "Bye, Mom. Bye, Dad."

"Good night, kids. Have fun," her mother said.

Her father shook his head, mumbling to himself, "Mike Kilpatrick? Where *have* I heard that name before?"

Scotti raised an eyebrow at the others as a

victory sign when they got into Mr. Markham's car. Lorna's father didn't know anything about the switch either, even though Scotti wondered if he thought it was strange that the two girls had traded boyfriends.

As soon as Mr. Markham dropped them off in front of the theater, all four burst out laughing.

"You should have seen it!" cried Mike. "It would have cracked you up!"

"Mike gave an Academy Award performance," said Scotti.

"Yeah, and her dad kept shaking his head and saying, 'Mike Kilpatrick? Where have I heard that name before?' " said Mike.

"Hey, everybody! Enough about that," Cary said excitedly. "Have I got a sur-*prise for you!*"

He grabbed Scotti and twirled her around. "Dad and I finished my car last night! We put the last piece on, and I shined it up. It's sitting in the garage raring to go!"

"Cary, that's terrific," said Scotti.

"Hey, man! Gimme a high-low," shouted Mike.

The boys slapped hands in the air above their heads and then down by their knees.

Laughing, Cary said, "That's not all. Wait'll you hear this! We're not going to the movie tonight. I made a deal with Rex. He's going to drive all of us to my house now, and we're going to take the car out for a little spin. After he and his girlfriend see the movie, he'll meet us at the house and bring us back to Rudy's so that we'll be where we're supposed to be when Mr. Markham picks us up. Is that a great plan or what?"

A thrill of excitement raced up Scotti's spine, but Lorna shot her a worried look.

"What about your parents?" asked Lorna. "Are they coming along?"

Cary burst out laughing. "Give me a break! Of course they aren't coming with us. They've gone over to some friends' house for dinner and a bridge game. They won't be home until after midnight. We'll be back way before that. There's no way they'll know we took the car."

"Sounds great to me," said Mike. He slipped an arm around Lorna. "We can go for a long drive in the country. We won't have to worry about somebody seeing us out there."

Scotti bit her lower lip as she listened to the others talk. As much as she was dying to ride in Cary's car, the idea was a little scary.

"What if something happens?" she asked. "We could get into a lot of trouble."

"Since when did you turn chicken?" Mike asked her. "I thought you were game for anything."

"What could go wrong? Absolutely nothing, that's what," argued Cary. "All the parts are brand-new. It even has new tires, so there's no chance we'll get a flat. Come on, everybody. Here comes Rex."

Cary and Mike hurried down the street toward a red convertible that was pulling up at the curb. Scotti and Lorna trailed behind.

"I don't know if this is such a good idea," said Scotti. "My dad would kill me if he ever found out."

"I don't think we should go," said Lorna. She stopped and put a hand on Scotti's arm. "They can go if they want to. You and I can go to the movie the way we planned, and they can meet us at Rudy's later. That way they can do their macho stuff, and we won't have to worry about getting in trouble."

Scotti didn't reply. She was watching Cary and Mike talk excitedly to Rex. Cary was motioning her toward him.

"Come on! We need to hurry," he insisted. "Rex and Sarah want to get back before the movie starts."

"Oh, Lorna! I don't know what to do! I want to go with Cary so badly, but . . ." She hesitated. It was as if two different movies were playing in her head. On one screen her father was reading her the riot act for going in a car with a teenage boy and grounding her until she graduated from college. But on the other screen, she was sitting beside Cary in the front seat of his Mustang. He had his arm around her, and the radio was turned up high. Outside the car, the countryside was racing by. It was wonderful! How could she possibly pass up such a chance?

"Come on, Lorna," she urged. "It'll be okay. Nothing bad will happen."

"But, Scotti—"

Scotti looked frantically at Lorna and then at the boys, who were motioning and calling to them to hurry.

"You can't go to the movie alone," said Scotti, grabbing Lorna's arm and pulling her along. "I promise you. Everything's going to be okay!"

A moment later the two couples had squeezed into the backseat of the convertible, heading toward Cary's house.

# 23

"**W**hat a beauty! Man, I'd give anything for a car like this!" exclaimed Mike the instant Cary opened the garage door, revealing the gleaming white Mustang.

"She's my masterpiece," Cary said proudly. He ran a finger lovingly across the hood. "I've been working on her for over three years."

Lorna couldn't help admiring the beautiful car, too. There wasn't a dent anywhere, and the chrome trim sparkled.

"It's really neat," she said.

"See, I told you you'd love this," Scotti reminded her. "We're going to have a *fantastic* time."

"Yeah," Mike said. He came up behind Lorna and wrapped his arms around her, whispering, "Aren't we, Lorna?"

She froze. She had been so busy worrying that someone might catch Cary driving illegally that she had forgotten about Mike and what a long ride in the country could mean.

"What's the matter?" he asked.

"Nothing," she replied, but deep down she knew this was it. Tonight she would have to make a decision she didn't want to make.

"The first rule is, nobody drools on my car."

Cary's voice interrupted her thoughts. He was rubbing an imaginary spot off the front fender with his shirtsleeve, making everyone laugh.

"What are we waiting for?" Scotti asked. "Let's go!"

Moments later they were backing out of the Calheims' driveway. In the backseat, Lorna was starting to relax. Mike had his arm draped loosely around her shoulder, but his attention was on the car.

"Would you listen to that engine purr," he said with admiration. "This is one sweetheart of a car."

They were heading north, away from the bright lights and heavy traffic. Cary had turned the volume up on the radio, and rock music throbbed from speakers behind Lorna's head. She didn't know when she'd felt so grown-up. This is fun, she admitted to herself. I was silly to have been so worried.

A little while later Cary turned off the main

road onto a dirt road. The sign at the turnoff said Grapevine Lake. Lorna had been to the lake dozens of times and she knew it was enormous. There were miles and miles of winding roads and not much civilization around it.

"Hey, guys. Do we really want to go back here?" she called out.

No one in the front seat seemed to hear her. Cary had his eyes on the road, and Scotti was singing with the radio.

Turning to Mike, she said, "I really think we should stay on the main road. I mean, what if we got lost back here?"

"There you go again, Lorna, worrying when you should just let Cary take care of the driving." He pulled her close and kissed her deeply.

Lorna couldn't help kissing him back. Being in his arms felt so good. But at the same time alarms were going off and her brain was telling her to be careful. She tried to push away from Mike.

"You know I really like you, don't you?" he whispered.

Lorna nodded. "And I like you, too, Mike. Really."

"Then loosen up a little. Okay? I'm not going to hurt you. I promise."

**152**

Lorna let him kiss her again. Maybe I should just trust him, she thought.

She put her head on his shoulder and tried to relax, but it was impossible. Her mind was reeling with questions, and the bumpy road was bouncing the car like a carnival ride.

Suddenly Lorna realized what was wrong. I'm totally miserable, she thought. I don't want to be in this car with Cary driving. And I don't want to spend all my time with Mike making out! This must be what Scotti meant when she said I wouldn't like myself if I did something I thought was wrong. Right now I don't like myself at all!

Just then Mike pulled her close again.

"Mike! Don't!" she cried, bolting out of his arms and scooting as far away from him as the tiny backseat would allow. "Don't do that. *Please!*"

"Aw, come on, Lorna," he pleaded. "It's okay."

"No, it isn't okay. Not with me," she insisted. "I want to go home."

He was staring at her so intently that she wanted to cry. I should never have gone out with him again, she thought miserably. It isn't worth it to lose my self-respect.

At that same instant she realized that the engine had stopped humming and the car was jerking forward, making little hops until it came to a stop.

"Cary, why are you stopping?" she demanded. "We're in the middle of nowhere!"

He didn't answer at first. Then he turned around, a sheepish look on his face.

"I blew it big time," he said, shaking his head. "There is one thing I forgot to do . . . get gas."

The only sound in the car was the disc jockey's voice coming out of the radio. "It's a quarter to ten on a rocking Friday night, people, and time to give a listen to the latest single from Mariah Carey."

Three pairs of eyes stared at Cary in horror.

# 24

"**I** guess there's nothing to do but walk back in the direction we came from," said Scotti.

They had gotten out of the car and were surveying the countryside. Moonlight splashed across the lake. In its glow they could see nothing but grassy land studded with clumps of trees.

"Do you remember passing a house since we turned off the highway?" asked Lorna.

"Or a gas station?" Mike asked urgently. "They'd have a phone, and we could call our parents and make up some big story about why we're going to be so late."

Cary shook his head sadly. "I haven't seen a single sign of civilization for miles. I'm sorry, guys. I don't know why I didn't think about getting gas while we were still in town. It was really stupid."

Scotti put a hand on Cary's arm. "You're

just not used to taking a car on long drives," she said. As scared as she was to face her parents, she couldn't help feeling sorry for Cary. For such a nice person, he was a walking disaster. No matter how hard he tried, everything he did came off wrong—especially if her father was involved.

"This is creepy," said Lorna. "Let's get out of here."

The two couples walked along the road in silence for the next few minutes. Scotti's insides were quivering as she thought about how angry her father was going to be. Even though she had told him that she was going to spend the night with Lorna, she was sure the Markhams would call her parents when Lorna's father couldn't find them at Rudy's after the movie.

That could be happening right now, she thought and quivered even harder.

"Scotti, I'll take full responsibility for this," Cary said.

He sounded nervous, and his voice startled her.

"I know your dad is probably going to kill me, but I'll make sure he knows that none of this was your fault."

Scotti sighed. "That's okay, Cary. It won't do any good. I've done two things that are going to land me in *deep* trouble. I lied about who I was going out with so I could be with you. And I rode in a car with a teenage boy. I'm doomed."

"I guess we both are, big time," he said, taking her hand. "My parents are probably going to forbid me to drive again until I get my license. At age eighteen. Or twenty-five. You know, Scotti, they might even take away my car!"

Lorna and Mike trudged along several yards behind Scotti and Cary. Lorna's eyes darted around warily. The bushes and trees beside the road made dark, eerie shapes, and she was alert to every sound. What if someone was hiding in the darkness? Waiting to pounce on them.

Lorna had read about things like that. Druggies who robbed people and even murdered them and left them in ditches. She shivered and moved closer to Mike.

To her surprise, he scowled and ducked away.

She stopped in the middle of the road and faced him squarely. "Are you still mad at me?" she asked indignantly.

He stopped, too, and his eyes flicked toward her, but he didn't answer.

"I don't believe you," she said incredulously. "Here we are, stuck out in the middle of nowhere with no way to get home, and you're mad be-

cause I wouldn't make out! We could be murdered out here, and if that doesn't happen, our
parents will probably kill us when we get home,
and you can't think about anything but—"

"Lorna, you don't understand," he interrupted. "It really hurts my ego the way you come
on to me so strong, making me think that you
really like me, and then stop me cold when I try
to show you how much I like you."

She couldn't believe what she was hearing.
"I do like you, but all you want is one thing. And
kissing is *not* the only way to show me you like
me. I'm not like that, and I can't figure out whatever made you want to go out with me in the first
place."

Mike shrugged. "I just liked you, that's all.
So many girls throw themselves at guys, but you
were different. You were cool. You were more
interesting because you were harder to get. And
the more I've gotten to know you, the better I like
you. You're fun. And sincere. At least I thought
you were sincere. But lately I've started thinking
that you don't really like me after all. You just get
a kick out of playing around with my feelings."

"Mike, that isn't true," she said. "I really *do*
like you. More than you know. You make me feel
so special. And if I've led you on and then
stopped you, it's because I've been trying to

make a decision for myself. Should I go further than I want to so that you won't dump me for someone like Holly Hooper? Or should I stop you when I don't feel comfortable anymore?" She paused and took a deep breath. "I guess I've just made my decision, Mike," she said softly. "If you can't be with me without getting carried away making out, then we shouldn't go out anymore. I like you, but I have to like myself."

Mike didn't reply. He stood there in the moonlight, looking into her eyes. She gazed back and listened to the crickets chirping in the grass, wondering if this was the end. If Mike was trying to find the words to tell her it was all over between them. Her heart was bursting.

"Hey, guys! What happened to you? Did you get lost?"

Cary's voice broke the spell. He and Scotti were racing toward them through the darkness.

"We found a phone!" Scotti said breathlessly. "There's a little grocery store up here. It's closed for the night, but the pay phone outside works. Cary's going to call Rex and tell him where we are and ask him to bring us a can of gas."

"Cool," said Mike. Then glancing toward Lorna, he added, "You guys go ahead and make the call. We'll catch up."

Lorna's heart thudded in her chest as Scotti and Cary disappeared in the darkness again. She looked up at Mike, dreading the words she knew he was about to say.

"I . . . I don't exactly . . . um . . . know how to say this," he began, fumbling the words.

Lorna fought to hold back tears.

"I'm really glad we talked this out, though, Lorna. I want you to know that I'd hate it if I made you feel bad about yourself," he said. "I like you too much to do a thing like that. I promise that I won't pressure you"—he ducked his head sheepishly and then grinned at her—"if you'll still be my girlfriend."

Lorna caught her breath. "YES!" she cried. "Yes, Mike, I *will* still be your girlfriend. I promise."

He kissed her softly, and they walked hand in hand down the deserted road.

I know I'm going to be in trouble when I get home, but if I can handle this, I can handle anything, she thought, feeling a sudden glow of pride.

# 25

Lights were blazing from every window when the white Mustang pulled into the Markhams' driveway. As Cary shut off the engine, the front door opened, and four men streamed onto the front porch and peered angrily into the darkness.

"Oh, my gosh! My dad's here!" cried Scotti, her heart stopping. "He's in his bathrobe!"

"Mine's here, too," said Cary.

"And mine," echoed Mike. "Looks like we're about to face a firing squad."

Scotti wished that she could disappear from the face of the earth. Her father looked as if he were about to explode.

She took a deep breath and opened the car door. "Come on, guys. Let's get this over with."

They got out of the car and shuffled toward

the house in a tight group, like four condemned prisoners.

"Scotti Wheeler! I want to know the meaning of this *this instant!*" her father demanded.

"Just a minute there. I want to talk to my son. Cary, what was the big idea of sneaking that car out behind our backs! Do you realize that you don't have insurance, much less a license to drive!" Mr. Calheim shouted angrily.

Mike's father pushed forward and yelled at his son, "This is the worst thing you've pulled in a long time, and you can bet there are going to be serious consequences."

Just then Scotti's father pointed a finger at Mike.

"Mike Kilpatrick. Now I know where I heard that name before. You're Lorna's boyfriend. I see what's going on now. You helped her sneak out behind my back to be with Cary! I won't stand for a thing like that!"

Mr. Kilpatrick shouted something back at Scotti's father, but Scotti couldn't hear what it was because now all the fathers were yelling.

Finally Mr. Markham held up his hand for quiet. "I think we'd better move inside the house. It's two in the morning, and the neighbors are liable to call the police and have us all arrested for disturbing the peace."

**162**

# THE GREAT DAD DISASTER

When they reached the living room, Scotti was surprised to see her mother sitting on the sofa. Mrs. Markham was there, too, along with two other women who she knew must be Cary's and Mike's mothers.

Lorna's father motioned to everyone to be seated. He turned to Lorna and said, "I want you to know how deeply disappointed I am in you. I thought you were mature and responsible enough to make your own decisions about your curfew. Obviously I was wrong. I never dreamed that you would do something as foolish as you did tonight. It breaks my heart to say this, but I'm going to have to be strict from now on."

Scotti didn't dare look at Lorna. She didn't dare look anywhere except at the floor. Her own father's next words startled her.

"And as for you, Cary Calheim, I demand to know why you *lured* my daughter off in your car when you knew that I specifically forbade her to get into cars with boys."

"Just a minute there, Mr. Wheeler," piped up Cary's father. "How dare you accuse my son of luring your daughter anywhere. She's been hanging around our garage, watching him work on that car for weeks. How do you know that *she* didn't lure *him* into sneaking it out of the garage and going for a ride? Answer that!"

*163*

Mr. Wheeler jumped to his feet. "Are you questioning the character of my daughter? My *little girl*? I won't stand for that!" He lunged for Mr. Calheim, who pulled back so suddenly that he rolled his chair over backward.

Scotti looked on in horror as her mother jumped up and raced toward the two men. What is she going to do? Scotti thought frantically. Are all the parents going to get into a fight?

"Shame on you two! You're behaving like adolescents!" said Mrs. Wheeler. "Let's think this through calmly."

Grumbling and frowning at each other, the two men got back to their seats. Scotti couldn't imagine what was going to happen next. Everyone in the room was on the edge of their chairs.

"What's the matter with all of you? Can't you see that every one of us here is partly to blame for what happened tonight?" Mrs. Wheeler said. "Naturally what the kids did was wrong. I'm not excusing them. But we've been wrong, too. Craig and I have been far too strict with Scotti. That's why she felt she had to sneak around."

"I agree with what you're saying," said Mrs. Markham. "It really wasn't fair to Lorna to give her so much responsibility at her age. We should have set limits instead of expecting her to be able to do it all by herself. Why, I remember that when I was dating, there were times I was thankful that I had a curfew to fall back on"—she chuckled and blushed slightly—"especially when Coy started to get too romantic."

Soft laughter rippled around the room, and Scotti noticed that Lorna's eyes were shining with happiness.

"I suppose we can all find room for improvement," said Mr. Calheim. "I'm just glad they're home safe and sound. You kids gave us quite a scare, you know."

Scotti breathed a huge sigh of relief. "And you'll never know how scared we were," she said. "None of us will *ever* do that again."

Mr. Wheeler looked at her tenderly. "Sounds like my little girl's growing up," he said, moisture filling his eyes.

Scotti ran to her father and hugged him, holding on as tightly as she could. She wanted to keep holding on forever. She knew she would probably be punished, and so would her friends, and Cary would go on messing up no matter how much she tried to defend him. But this was an extra special moment between her and her dad. Things were going to get better.

# 26

Lorna was waiting for Scotti to call when the phone rang at exactly six-thirty sharp. They had talked on the phone at that same time every day for the past twenty-nine days. Today was day thirty.

"Are you ready?" Scotti asked excitedly.

"You bet!" Lorna replied.

"On your mark," said Scotti.

"Get set," said Lorna.

"*Go!*" they cried in unison.

Lorna made a giant X over the day's date on her calendar. "I can't believe it," she cried into the phone. "It's finally over."

"Me either. When our parents agreed to ground all four of us for a whole month, I never thought I'd make it," said Scotti. "And poor Cary. He's not only grounded, he's lost his driving privileges for six months."

# THE GREAT DAD DISASTER

"You never thought *you'd* make it," said Lorna. "The night we got grounded was the same night I finally worked things out with Mike. Now I've had to wait a whole month to go out with him again. You know, Scotti, I just wish I'd taken your advice sooner and leveled with him about how I felt."

"The important thing is that you didn't let things go too far," said Scotti. "Now when you go out with Mike tomorrow night you won't have a problem."

"Boys!" said Lorna. "Let's face it, we were right when we said boys *are* the problem. Everything in our lives changed when boys got into the picture."

"I know. If it hadn't been for boys our friendship wouldn't have been in trouble," added Scotti.

"Yeah, and if it hadn't been for boys we wouldn't have had problems *big time* with our dads," said Lorna.

"It's all working out okay, though," said Scotti. "You and I are best friends again. And Dad is even loosening up a little. He's letting me go to Rudy's with Cary and you and Mike for a little while tomorrow night, even though it's a school night."

"My dad's given me a curfew, but that's

okay. I might need it in case Mike forgets about our little talk," Lorna said, laughing.

Scotti giggled. "Speaking of our dads, you'll have to admit that the funniest sight you ever saw in your life was all four of our fathers on your front porch in the middle of the night. And mine was in his pajamas!"

"It was a riot!" agreed Lorna.

And they laughed and laughed and laughed.

After they hung up, Scotti opened her diary.

*Dear Diary,*

*This is probably my last entry for a while. I'm going to be busy writing another novel. It will be about all the experiences Lorna, Mike, Cary, and I just had and how they changed our lives.*

*I'm going to call it THE GREAT DAD DISASTER.*

# About the Author

BETSY HAYNES is the author of more than fifty novels for young people including the Taffy Sinclair books, The Fabulous Five series, *The Great Mom Swap, The Great Dad Disaster,* and *The Great Boyfriend Trap.* Her other books include award-winners *Cowslip* and *Spies on the Devil's Belt.* When she isn't writing, Betsy loves to read mysteries and to travel, and she and her husband Jim spend as much time as possible aboard their boat, *Nut & Honey.*

The Hayneses live on Marco Island, Florida, and have two grown children, two keeshond dogs, and a black cat with extra toes.